INFINITY

INFINITY

Love Vs Fate

EISHITA

PARTRIDGE

A Penguin Random House Company

To order additional copies of this book, contact
Partridge India
000 800 10062 62
orders.india@partridgepublishing.com

www.partridgepublishing.com/india

TO
THE BEAUTIFUL STREETS OF
LONDON AND *LOS ANGELES*.

PREFACE

Hi there, I am Eishita, the author of the book you are about to read. I am a die-hard fan of a British-Irish boy band called 'One Direction' and Durjoy Datta, I am a reading aficionado; 'The Fault in Our Stars', 'I Too Had a Love Story 'and 'Can Love Happen Twice?' are some of the books, I would love to marry soon.

'Infinity' is second my book to get published.

I wrote this book when I was twelve. Yes, this is older than my first book but got published later. 'Writing' is a loved hobby in my house. My family includes a bunch of beautiful yet unpublished writers. I was inspired to write and get my work published in order to make my family proud of me. Since I have discovered my passion for words, pen and paper, it does not let me sleep in peace.

Dear Reader, The creation of this book was a turning point for me; as I analyzed human nature and the way a person reacts while sketching characters. Writing brings about a new person in me at the end of each book. Due to it I have become more sensible and have started to behave a bit (emphasis on bit) mature.

After *"How Could I Not See Him?"* that was my first book, a romance. *"Infinity"* is a different love story with lots of twists and turns. I am thankful to you for buying it, taking out time from your busy schedule and reading it. It would make me happy if you go ahead, buy the other book and recommend that/this to your friends if you like it.

No offence is intended to anyone, this book is a pure work of fiction and things are included due to the need of the hour. No personal hatred to any person, place or religion.

It would make my day if you drop your messages, appreciations and questions as Direct Messages on Twitter, Instagram and Facebook. Also, if you like my page as soon as you finish reading; I would love to respond to your messages. Constructive criticism and love is forever welcome.

I hope you enjoy it!

HAPPY READING!

ACKNOWLEDGEMENT

I would like to express my gratitude to the many people who helped me grow in the formative years of my life, provided support, room for exchanging views, outlooks, appreciation, criticism and to all those who assisted in the editing, proof-reading and designing.

This book is a gift to my late grandmother Mrs. Bimla Shukla. I would also take this moment to thank my maternal grandfather, Mr. G.P. Dwivedi. This is for their showers of immense love, support and blessings from up where they reside and belong, paradise.

It is also dedicated to the streets of London, Los Angeles and Bradford; the places where some parts of the story are set.

I would also thank my parents, Mrs. Pallavi Asheesh and Mr. Asheesh Misra, for bringing me into this world, and for their endless support and unconditional love. Without them, I do not think I and this book would have been where we are, today. Thank you for showing your endless support, interest in my work, believing in me and helping me to achieve my dream.

A token of gratitude to my sister Aishwarya Misra for helping me through all these years and my friend Unnati Jain for helping me with some lyrics.

I would love to thank my friends and my proof-readers, Priyanshi Bhakuni, Anushka Kudesia, Simantika Chanchani and Suryanshi Anand for reading my write ups and stories. I want to put up a special mention to my two best friends and also my best supporters, Arushi Kanojia and Vidhi Saxena.

I love you all so much.

And, I obviously *have* to thank the Partridge India Family. Thank you for standing by me through this amazing phase of book publishing. It has been a great experience with them and their dedicated consultants who have not only designed the cover and helped me with my book, but also have answered the endless amounts of questions.

Last but not the least; I would love to give a massive thank you to my Wattpad family aka my readers on Wattpad who have always rose up my moral level and encouraged me to keep writing. I do not think I would have written this book without your incredible support. Thank you tons everyone!

EISHITA...

PROLOGUE

<u>Scarlette</u>

"Yes baby where is your mumma? I smiled, fixing her braid weakly.

"She is with dad. She told me to leave them alone a little bit." She pouted cutely.

"Aww! And where is Ada aunt?" I asked her.

She tilted her head, "Ada aunt has gone out with her kitty party friends." She pouted again.

"Aww my poor baby left all alone? Hahaha come here." I giggled.

"No I'm going to stay with grand dad!" She stuck her tongue out at me and ran towards him.

He high fived her little hands and winked at me "See Scarlette? She wants to stay with me. Now you be jealous!"

I just laughed and looked at my wheelchair for a while, then posed my head on his shoulder silently.

"Alright Maria look who is here! Go play with her!" He pointed at Maria's best friend Angela.

She giggled "okay!" and ran away.

Chapter 1

"Scarletttttee!!!!" I heard an irritating and shrill voice shout that my mind registered was my younger sister Ellie's. "What the *fuck* is your problem Ellie?" I murmured in my pillow, "Stop cursing early in the morning Scarlette!" Mum scolded me.

I groaned loudly and sat up, "What is the issue that is making you shout like a wild animal in the middle of an apocalypse Ms. Ellie John Waters?" I asked batting my eyelashes innocently as a yawn escaped my mouth.

"If you were to be selected as a stylist you were to get a call letter today, right?" She asked me with excited eyes mentioning to the job for which I had applied at the Carter Music Management office last week.

I nodded with crossed fingers and closed eyes, "They loved your fashion sense Scarlette! You are the official stylist for Groove from this minute!" She yelled at the top of her voice.

"What? They assigned *me* as a stylist for *Groove*, seriously? The biggest boy band on the planet!" I asked with my jaw on the floor and eye balls literally popping out of my eye sockets.

"Yes Miss Scarlette John Waters! You are the stylist for Groove. You will be joining work from tomorrow that is why I was yelling!!" She said and the next thing I knew was that I was engulfed in bear hugs from mum and her.

I snatched away the call letter from her, it said-

"*To Ms. Scarlette John Waters,*

We would love to inform you that we have found the correct amount of depth in your styling that is needed to style a popular boy band. Therefore, we assign you as the designer of one of the bands managed by us, Groove.

The band consists of five boys, Mark James Merchant, Oliver James Edwards, Jacob San Tiago, Shawn William Cordan and Abraham Yaser Khan. We would appreciate if you join work from tomorrow.

Remember once you join work from tomorrow you cannot quit while the boys are on tour i.e. for eight months straight.

Sincerely,

Peter Devine (CARTER MUSIC Management)

So yeah, hi! I am Scarlette John Waters from London; I have pursued my fashion designing (with a gold medal though) from National Institute of Fashion and Arts. My family is only my mother June Mary Waters and my younger sister Ellie 'El' John Waters.

My mum brought us up facing a lot of troubles because our so called 'father', Mr. John Casper Waters, left us and ran away when I was 2 years old and Ellie was just born. Due to this marvelous act of bravery by him, I need to work to support Ellie's education and other family expenses along with my expenses.

We live in a not so grand house but because it is complete so I do not complain. There is no use of having a luxurious life if one cannot sit and have one time food with their family. I have a small room upstairs just next to Ellie's while mum sleeps downstairs having her room next to the kitchen.

I am expected to behave properly as houses in my colony are quite close to one another. But currently, I am jumping really high in my room due to the news Ellie just broke.

I have a heart shaped face that perfectly frames my wide, black eyes. I have wavy brown hair, shoulder length; though it depend my mood, I dye them black too. They begin straight and then at the end they get wavy naturally. I am 5'5 and I have a slim body with long legs. I do not like my nose as it is the button kind that turns up slightly when I find something cute or something that pisses me off. The 'kind' that never sticks out in a crowd.

Maybe if I believe people I can be called a pretty person. I read those books that you have never heard off, wedged in the trickiest places in the library. I am the chirpy, non-grown up 21 year old girl for whom 21 is literally a number. My clothes consist of a lot of colors. You say a color and you will find it in my wardrobe, not of big brands but yeah, good ones. Most of the times, when not at home, I tie my hair in a ponytail or a bun. Other than this they are left loose.

I am a different type of shy, I am not loud in first meeting but after that you can never shut me up. I am a girl hidden behind a big mask, hiding hundreds of tears and secrets behind a big grin. I never speak my mind, but rather I love expressing myself. I have a fear for just about everything, especially boys with angelic faces, and small places. The personality does however, mingle a lot with music.

If you need me to be I can be serious although I act childish most of the time. And also I will have cravings and if you know what is good for you, you will deal with it. If you are my friend then I love you to bits and pieces because I am very choosy about my friends. Although friendly with everyone because it just hurts to, hurt someone else.

Shaking my thoughts away, I got up from my bed and freshened up. I hopped in for a nice, long, warm and luxurious shower. I let the warm water run through my body, relaxing and soothing it down. After having a nice bath I changed into my Green tank top and denim hot pants.

I went down for breakfast, it smelled amazing today. The day in my 'palace' looks beautiful, today. Bacons, cheese sandwiches and orange juice! What was today? Christmas? No, it was like last month. I mentally went through my, mom and Ellie's birthday but none of it was today. I was so surprised to not find the usual sandwich and milk but this, not that I detest such kind of meal but still.

I yelled to mum, "Mum what it is today? Such amaazziiinngg food?"

I heard her chuckle, "You got a job love." Wait, this was all she replied? Unable to understand I shrugged it off, sat on the chair and switched on my phone as I waited for them.

"Two mails, two missed calls and three whatsapp messages." Too much popularity today. I opened the call log and saw that both the calls had been made from the same unknown number.

I dialed them, "Hello? I got a call from this number, an hour back. May I know who it is?" I asked, "Um, Hi! Maybe Peter would have called you back then! I do not know. I will tell him, you called when he is back." The other person replied in a heavy British accent and angelic voice, "Um okay. May I know which place is that?" I asked, he seemed to snort, Carter Music Management office." He replied rudely, "Ca-Carter Music office? Oh I am the new stylist." I informed him, "So?" He replied back in a rude tone, "Tell him I had called and my name is Scar-" the phone disconnected.

The person was such a rude soul, not even knowing how to behave with a person who is calling for the first time. People who are rude to someone for no reason but because they themselves are rude irritate me to death. They are one of the few things or people that raise my temper, or otherwise I am a very calm soul. Without knowing the face I knew who this person was, the man with a sexy accent, lovely voice, proud attitude and stone heart, the one and only Abraham Yaser Khan. I already know I would not have a great time with him being the poles apart kind of people we were.

After having a nice, lazy breakfast a few minutes later my phone rang, "Hello, Scarlette John Waters. Who is this?" I asked as I picked up the unknown number call, "Hello Ms. Scarlette. I am Peter Devine from the Carter Music Management office." The person on the other line said in a strict business tone. Peter Devine? Who? Oh shoot! It took me a few minutes to connect Peter Devine with Carter Music Management and reason for the call.

I gasped inside; the *Peter Devine* has called me. I did a little dance at my uncontrollable delight.

"Ms. Waters?" He asked. Realizing I had not uttered a word, "Yeah sorry! Scarlette here." I replied. "I believe you got the call letter already Miss?" He asked, "Yes sir." I smiled, "Good, you have to join as the stylist for the band Groove from tomorrow. I hope you know that?" He asked me, "Yes sir. I will be there at the office by 10am." I replied.

"Good. You have to go on tour with the boys as well for a good eight months. You must know that. Now, will you?" He asked me with a hint of uncertainty in his voice, I knew this already and spoken and got permission from my mother while breakfast.

"Yes sir, I will." I replied back confidently, "Just that I need to know them a bit before touring the world. If you know what I mean?" I stated my condition.

"Yes Miss Waters, one month you will be working with the boys in London and then we would start the WHILE WE ARE tour." He informed me, "You will be paid 40,000 dollars a month. Are you ready?" He asked me, "Yes Sir!" I replied. "Welcome to the CARTER MUSIC management Scarlette! Ok then, see you soon. Bye" He said and disconnected the call.

I nodded in agreement and grinned like a complete fool, tomorrow is going to be *such* an interesting day.

Chapter 2

<u>Scarlette</u>

I woke up at five in the morning without an alarm, but being lazy as hell, I kept lying down in my bed, counting the minutes till seven I drifted off to sleep again.

At seven, my phone alarm sung the new Groove single, No Control. I quickly hopped into shower and washed my hair. I *had* to look presentable today. I quickly changed into my blue and white plaid shirt and khaki jeans paired with my black pumps. I straightened my hair and left them loose.

I had to go to the *Carter Music Management Office* today.

I took off my footwear and went to the small statue of Jesus Christ kept in one corner of my little room and kneeled down in front of him, "Lord! All these 21 years of living you have given me so much in life. You also took away few things but I do not want them back. I have got no reason to. Help me manage this job well lord. Not for me, but for mum and Ellie. Amen." I read some Bible verses and lighted the candle.

Panicking as I checked the time I marched down the stairs and wished my mum, "Morning mum!" I said and kissed her cheeks, "Morning!" She replied. "Prayed?" She asked, "Mom do you even *need* to ask Scarlette John Waters if she has prayed or not? She *always* prays before stepping out of the house." Ellie poked her nose and said in a 'that is obvious' tone. I rolled my eyes at her and nodded at mum after which she flashed her pretty smile.

I picked up a toast and mum's car keys to drive to the office, "Eat at least child." She said to me, I waved the toast and gave her a flying kiss.

"Scarlette do not tell anyone anything there." She told me in a worried tone referring to some things that have changed our lives totally. "I will never do that mum. No one would get *that* close to me." I replied biting my lip, "You never know Scarlette, anything can happen." Ellie said in a serious tone, I shook my head and sighed, "Anyways, all the best!" She came over and hugged me being the angel she is, mum also hugged me and I went out.

The cold breeze hit my face, I stuffed my hands into my jeans pockets and hopped into mum's dirty second hand Dacia Sandero and sighed, mum was talking nonsense. None of the boys or anyone will get *that* close to me that I tell them things about my past and future, I would be my chirpy usual self but will always have a shell around me. No one would be that close to me, I know that.

Little did I know that this job would bring my life upside down and make me want things back that God took away from me a long time back.

My phone rung breaking my chain of thoughts, *Augustus calling* the screen flashed. I clapped; a best friend is all what you need at times, "Hi Augusieee!" I yelled in a stupid tone, he chuckled at it as usual, "Hi Scarrrr!!!" He replied back in my tone. "What's up boi?" I asked him, "Nothing. I am in a bit hurry, just called to wish you all the best love. I got a meeting. Will surely talk later. Bye!" He said hurriedly and disconnected the call.

I sighed in despair; I needed to talk to him a bit. Understanding that his job was also important, I shrugged it off.

I drove off to the office playing *Good for Him by Meleni Homez*; I parked my car into the parking next to a sexy looking jeep and a Porsche.

"Scarlette John Waters, new stylist, Groove." I said proudly to the guard, he checked his register and lead me to a huge building, "This way miss," he pointed to a big cabin door, *Peter Devine*, the name plate flashed in a golden italic font.

"We were expecting you. Mister Devine has been waiting for you, have a good day madam." He wished me and went off to his duty. I took a deep breath, straightened my shirt and ran fingers through my hair.

I knocked on the glass door, "Who is it?" I voice boomed from inside, a voice I had heard hundreds of times judging participants at different music reality shows. "Um… the new stylist?" I said, "We were expecting you miss. Please come in." He said and I crept in.

There he was with his white V-neck and I swear I could see some chest hair popping out of there. He was looking at a paper and the Groove boys were sitting around.

"Good morning Sir," I wished him with a warm smile as I interrupted him; he looked up and lowered the paper to have a clear view of me. He then plastered a smile, "Good Morning miss."

I glanced at the five handsome boys staring at me whom I had seen a lot of times on my Tumblr account oh and even Twitter, "Hi, how are you guys?" I asked them, "Hello love. We are great. What about you?" Oliver Edwards, in a black shirt and blue jeans, being the humble man he is asked me, "I am good, thank you." I smiled at them.

I could see Abraham Khan; he was older to me, and he was around 23 while I was just 21. He was sitting in a white t-shirt and black pants, staring at me in a weird way, I shrugged off. "Please have a seat, lady" Jacob San Tiago, the cute and curly boy in maroon T-shirt and grey jeans said. I nodded as I looked for seats, there was only one seat. Next to…*Abraham*!

I mentally groaned and sat down next to him without looking at him directly but sideways I could see him staring at a girl's picture in his phone. The good thing was Jacob sitting on the other side and I guess he was a nice person.

"So listen," Peter diverted all the attention, "Scarlette is your n-" he stopped midway and was eyeing Abraham who was staring at his phone, "Abraham leave the room," he said strictly, he seemed to be startled at his words, "Sorry what?" He said blinking his eyes as he stood up.

"I said *leave* the room this very moment." He repeated again, Abraham looked horrified at this, "B-but why?" He asked, "Because you are busy fucking girls and staring at their nudes so much that you do not have time for a meeting." A hard taunt hit his face; he looked down, "I am sorry." He mumbled to which Peter nodded and let him sit.

I noticed Abraham stealing glances at me all through the time, "Scarlette Waters is your new stylist. One month here and then on the While We Are tour. Be good." He said and Jacob turned to me, "Congratulations." He let out his hand and I shook it with a warm smile. From the side I also noticed Oliver giggling like a schoolgirl.

Peter stood up and others too followed, "Any issues?" He looked at us with raised eyebrows, "Is she official designer? Like, after While We Are too?" Abraham asked plainly, "Yes. She is brilliant." Peter replied, Abraham looked down and snorted as I frowned at him.

"Anything else?" He asked, "I start today?" I asked him, "No. It is an off for these dorks," he said and the four boys pouted, and because Groove did it…it had to be cute.

"You may start tomorrow. Meeting is over" he said and shook hands with me. "Welcome and congratulations." Mark shook hands with me and so did the others except for Abraham who stood their looking at his phone.

I got blended with everyone specially Jacob, Shawn and everyone else except for Abraham as he just stood alone using his phone.

"Scarlette?" Jacob called me, "Would you like… um you know accompany me for a dinner tonight?" He asked hesitantly, "Are you asking me for a date?" I asked him with a smirk and crossed arms.

He looked down as he grew red, "Yeah, maybe…kind of." He bit his lip that I found extremely cute, "Sure then." I smiled as he widened his eyes, "Oh um I t-thought other way." He chuckled.

I turned around to check on the others but found only Abraham who was staring at us with a hard expression and I do not know how I stared back at him, "Scarl?" Jacob called me unsurely; I smiled at the nickname, "Jac." I replied back and he revealed his cute dimples.

"I will pick you at 8." He asked, "You do not have my address." I sighed he shut his eyes tight, "Text it to me." He replied, I sighed "You do not have my number." I said and received the same reaction, "Give me your number I will text you." He said.

I gave him my number, "Nice way of asking for numbers. I like it." I said in an approving tone and he laughed a bit, "At least I impressed you *a bit*." I stuck my tongue at him.

My mind was stuck to Abraham, I turned and our eyes were locked again, I was pretty sure I lost somewhere between reality and his eyes. "Will you accompany us?" Jacob tapped my shoulder spoke breaking the contact, mentioning to the boys in the jeep I shook my head, "Have some work at home. I will catch you later." I replied and his face fell a little but he nodded.

He took me by surprise as he engulfed me in a big and tight hug; I smiled and tiptoed as I hugged him. Then I realized, he was so tall and handsome as hell, he was around 6 ft 3 inches or something and I was just 5 ft 5 inches.

He pulled back as Oliver honked and smirked naughtily at him, inside joke maybe. "Great meeting. Will meet today. Bye." I said to him, "I am looking forward to today's *date.*" He said with a naughty expression and I nodded with raised eyebrows.

I turned back again and saw Abraham staring angrily at my and Jacob's intertwined fingers that I did not realize he did while talking. Being unable to understand Abraham, I shrugged off the thoughts and went off to the driving lot.

Jacob and Oliver were whispering to each other as they had not left because Mark had a call to attend and drive, I walk past them and they were quite.

I ignored this weird behavior and drove off home raising the volume of Gotta Be You that I did not know why reminded me of Abraham.

Chapter 3

<u>Abraham</u>

Flashback

We were sitting in Peter's office waiting for our new stylist who called yesterday and I had picked up her call. S... something was her name that I do not remember, *fine*, I did not care to even hear it yesterday.

There was a knock on the glass door of the cabin, "Who is it?" Peter asked, "Um...the new stylist?" the female voice jingled in an asking way, even though I have separated myself from these attractions but I was eager from within to know how the owner of this voice looked like.

"We were expecting you miss. Come in." He said and the voice got a figure.

I nearly fell down from my seat on looking at the beautiful girl in a blue and white plaid shirt with khaki pants. She looked so much like…Sarah. *My* Sarah. The only girl I *ever fell* for, the only girl that had made me cry, Sarah Zaidi. My cousin, my lover, my betrayer.

"Good morning Sir," She wished him with a warm smile that reminded me of Sarah's, she glanced at us who were staring at her, "Hi, how are you guys?" She asked, "Hello love. We are great. What about you?" Oliver being the pretentious humble man he is asked her in his fake gentleman tone, "I am good, thank you." She smiled at us.

I guess she could see me staring at her and appear like a total desperate but little did I care of all that, eventually she shrugged it off, "Please have a seat," Jacob butted in wishing her and trying to play his charm on her in order for his next prey, she nodded looking for seats, there was only one seat. Next to…me!

She sat down next to me without looking but I did not care because I was too busy admiring Sarah's picture on my phone.

I still remember that night, 3 years back.

Flashback

"I am sorry Abraham but you are not the reason for the things I have been blaming you for." Sarah hiccupped; her beautiful face was all red and swollen. I looked into her bloodshot eyes that were filled with guilt.

"Who did this Sarah if it was not me?" I asked her on the verge of tears, she sobbed and wiped her eyes, "The person who ruined me is no one else but R-"

Peter's booming voice shook me out of my thoughts as he said something strictly that I could not follow, "Sorry what?" I said blinking my eyes as I stood up.

"I said *leave* the room this very moment.» He repeated again, I was horrified at this, «B-but why?" I asked like a fool. "Because you are busy fucking girls and staring at their nudes so much that you do not have time for a meeting." A hard taunt hit my face, even though I was burning inside yet looked down, "I am sorry." I mumbled to which Peter nodded and let me sit as if it was a big favor.

I was stealing glances at the girl I could not keep my eyes off all through the time, "Scarlette Waters," she got a name now, "Is your new stylist. One month here and then on take me home tour. Be sweet." He said and I wanted to bang my head, she reminded me of Sarah, being on the tour would increase my emotional and anger breakouts.

Jacob turned to her, "Congratulations." He let out his hand and she shook with a warm smile but I only noticed Oliver giggling like a schoolgirl and understood that they were together up to no good; they have not done any good with their so called *"sweetness".*

Peter stood up and others too followed, "Any issues?" He looked at us with raised eyebrows, "Is she the official designer? Like, after While We Are also?" I blurted out plainly but regretted it soon because it came out very rude, "Yes. She is brilliant." Peter replied, to appear rude like I do I look down and snorted as she frowned.

"Anything else?" He asked, "I start today?" She asked him, "No. It is an off for these dorks," he said making the four boys pout, and me roll my eyes.

"You may start tomorrow. Meeting is over" he said and shook hands with her. "Welcome and congratulations." Mark shook hands with her and so did the others except for me as I was too engulfed with stopping my tears to spill in front of all of them, staring at Sarah's photos.

"Scarlette?" Jacob called her, "Will you like um you know accompany me for the dinner tonight?" He asked in a fake hesitant way, I so knew this was going to happen. His words hit me so hard on the face, "Are you asking me for a date?" She asked him with a hot smirk and crossed arms.

How could he ask her out on a date? She's not made for him! How can she be so casual? Wait, why am I thinking all this? Am I...*jealous*? Maybe! Why?

He looked down and he grew red as he always does, "Yea, maybe...kind of." He bit his lip, "Sure then." She smiled as he and this time I widened my eyes along with Jacob, "Oh um I t-thought other way." He chuckled. Another big slap of jealousy slapped me super hard because I felt as if someone was asking Sarah all this.

Suddenly she turned around and caught me staring at them with a hard expression and I do not know how and why she stared back at me. Even though I had promised myself I would never get attracted towards any other girl but Sarah, something changed in me. Something that never wanted me to look away, something that wanted me to just look at her forever.

"Scarl?" Jacob called her unsurely; she turned to him and smiled at the nickname while I wanted to stab him to death, "Jac." She replied back smiling and causing explosions in the deepest pits of my stomach.

"I will pick you at 8." He asked, there he goes, his usual way of asking for numbers, he is surely up to no good at all.

"You do not have my address." She sighed innocently and he shut his eyes tight pretending as if he never realized it, "Text me." He replied, both of us sighed at the same time "You do not have my number." He faked the same reaction with perfection, "Give me your number I will text you." He said.

Go to the acting industry Jacob San Tiago, I so wanted to shout on his face.

She gave him her number and this surprised me that she did not understand all this was pre rehearsed, "Nice way of asking for numbers. I like it." She said in an approving tone and quickly proved me wrong, "At least I impressed you a bit." He said flirtingly and she stuck her tongue out at him in the same cute way as Sarah used to do.

She turned back again and our eyes were locked in the deepest stare again as I drowned in her black eyes, "Will you accompany us?" Jacob tapped her shoulder and spoke breaking the most beautiful eye contact, mentioning to the boys in the car, she shook her head, "Have some work at home. I will catch you later." She replied and his face fell a little in the same way as his face always does but nodded.

He took me and maybe her also by surprise as he engulfed her in a big and tight hug, she smiled and tiptoed hugging him, reducing my patience level even more at Jacob's PDA.

He pulled back as Oliver honked and smirked naughtily at him, they had already talked about it. "Great meeting. Will meet today. Bye." She said to him, "I am looking forward to today's *date*." He said with a naughty expression and she nodded with an amazed expression.

My eyes fled to her fingers intertwined with Jacob's and I never had felt so angry for any girl other than Sarah. I looked up and saw her looking at me with a confused expression, seeing me trying to judge her expression she quickly went off to the driving lot.

I went to the washroom and into a cubicle crying quietly to myself, missing Sarah more than anything in the world. The taste of her lips on the top of my tongue was on the top of the list of the things I wanted at that point of time.

I got up realizing that anyone could see me here and wiped my eyes. I quietly yet quickly walked to the empty parking lot that was as empty as my life and heart.

I cried and punched a wall next to me continuously causing my knuckles to bleed and walls go red. I hopped in my car, all my heart drenched with pain and tears while my brain was filled with happy and sad memories but amidst all this realization hit me that I had not got over Sarah, as yet.

I shook off my thoughts and taking a deep breath I started my Porsche as the engine roared I looked out to notice that it was raining. I like rain because it tells us it is okay to cry sometimes because even the sky does.

I came on the main road, the silence in the car was deafening hence I raised the volume of the radio to hear Gotta Be You that also raised the pain in my chest.

When I did not believe in love, God sent Sarah, an angel for me who changed me forever. Then when I fell for her, he threw us apart.

When I was just trying to get over and forget Sarah forever he sent a girl exactly like her.

Why!? Am I a toy? To play with and make it cry or happy whenever you want? I cursed God for the first time in my life, in my most vulnerable and devastated situation.

"I miss you and I love you Sarah Zaidi. I will never replace you," I whispered to myself. Little did I know destiny had some other plans in her kitty for me.

Chapter 4

<u>Scarlette</u>

I reached home after a tough drive amidst rain and traffic, I stood out, taking everything in and enjoying the rain. "Scarlette! Come on get in, you will fall sick." Ellie came running out and pulled me inside.

I laughed as I went with her, "How were those Groove boys? And oh, Peter Devine?" Mum shot questions at me, "They are very nice and Peter is his usual self. All bossy, strict and business type." I replied casually, "I have to go get ready and will not eat at home today." I said and started going up to my room.

"May I ask why so, Ms. Waters?" Mum asked, I knew this was coming, I went down slowly, "Um, mum I-" I thought for a nice excuse, "Wait! You are going for a date?" Ellie spoke up, reading my mind. Mum raised her eyebrows as I nodded sheepishly, "With whom?" She asked curiously.

"That singer from Groove, Jacob San Tiago." I said in a low volume, "Jacob freaking San Tiago asked *you* for a *date*?" Ellie squealed like a fan girl.

"Ellie Waters stop behaving like a typical teenage fan girl." I said sternly, "I *am* a teenager. I am nine*teen*." She stated crossing her arms, instead of replying to her I looked over to mum, "Yea. We are going on a…date." I looked down.

Mum was about to hug me but stopped seeing me dripping, "I wish I could hug you. Anyways, good luck. Should I help you with the dress?" Her eyes brightened up, "Uhm. Okay." I nodded.

She quickly went in and came out with a Coco Channel packet, "Mum? Coco Channel? For us this is as costly as a plot in heaven or…Mars!" I gasped. She rolled her eyes, "When I was 25 Mister Waters…I mean your dad took me for a date. I was pregnant with Ellie and you were with your granddad at home. He gifted me this dress and told me; whenever Scarlette goes on her first date give her this dress. He-he was attached with you Scarlette." She sighed, I gave her a disappointed face. "Just keeping promises!" She said.

Mum thinks dad surely had some problems hence he went away. She cannot accept the fact that dad or I should say Mister John Casper Waters left us because of my illness and that he could not bring up two daughters that too, one problem stuck.

I sighed, "Mum I will not wear *anything* related to that man. If he was attached he would have stayed with us…not running away leaving you, me and Ellie at midnight in a hospital without even a goddamn explanation!" I gulped hard.

She looked down, "For me Scar?" She asked in a low tone. Oh my God that tone and that puppy face! They can make me do *anything* and when I say anything, I mean it. I nodded, "Fine! Just for this one, single time!" I took the packet and went up to my room.

I dried myself up; soon looking up at the clock I panicked a little, "Ellie! Can I borrow your wedges? It is already 5:30." I shouted and pleaded, "Fine. Do not break them." She said casually.

I quickly hopped in for a shower, undressing, I let the warm water flow on my body, radiating all the anger and anxiety in me. I wish I die soon. I sighed.

Suddenly I realized it was already 6:30pm I quickly wiped myself and put on my robe. Going outside, I felt my body cool down.

I picked up the packet and took out the dress, it was yellow, beautiful and ended on my mid thighs, it complemented my curves, as if it was meant to be for me. I put it on. I posed a bit in front of the mirror and put on a white pendant and a pink lip stain with kohl and a thin liner. Not over doing it.

My phone rang, *"Jacob San Tiago"* the caller ID flashed. I picked it up, "Ready love?" He asked, I sighed at the flirting, "Yeah love." I said imitating the way he said love. "Come out then" he said and disconnected the call.

I went down quietly, "Scarlette my baby! You look...like Selena Gomez!" Mum cooed, I rolled my eyes. "Yeah mum. Bye now. Love you." I said closing the door behind me.

"Scarlette!" Jacob exclaimed, leaning cross armed on his black limo. He looked hot in an off white shirt, black skin tight jeans and brown boots.

"Jacob!" I imitated his accent, he frowned, "Are you *always* this trashy? Or today is some special day?" He asked.

"No not at all, I am the same always." I smiled.

He took me by surprise again as he hugged me and I smelled his strong cologne. Pulling back he opened the door for me and I thankfully sat in.

He stopped at a restaurant named, *Regret Having No More.* I frowned at the name and looked at Jacob, "What?" He asked.

"Weird named restaurant" I raised my eyebrows.

"They change the name every week with such names but have great food. It is said that most people who come here realize these names come true in their lives. I do not know...let us try." He explained.

Okay, this place is strange. They change names every week and those things happen in the lives of the guests. Weird as fuck! I shrugged knowing that I am not going to regret whatever I do not have. I *thought*.

Jacob tapped my shoulder, "It is okay. They have great food. If you want we will go somewhere else?" He questioned, I shook my head even though I felt very anxious on the inside, "No it is okay." I said and linked my arms with him.

Smiling he went to the reception, "Hey sweetheart." He leaned on the table, the sexy receptionist was in a sky blue shirt, curly hair, tight black pencil fit skirt and round glasses.

"Y-Yes sir?" She asked, taken aback slightly with his sudden flirting.

"Got a booking?" He asked, his voice that clearly had pun intended, the girl smirked, "Got no booking. You can wait till tomorrow?" She said teasingly.

I winced; he had brought me on a date and was making fuck plans with a receptionist, that too in my presence.

I cleared my throat, "Hi fuck buddies! Done with your make out and hangout plans so can we eat? I am hungry!" I said in a pissed off tone, he rose his eyebrows at my choice of words while the girl flinched.

"Yeah okay." He smirked, "Sweetie. Jacob San Tiago." He winked, she pretended searching. A horrible thing followed, she held his hand that was on her cheek, and stroked it from her cheek to her breasts to her navel.

I stared at him; he noticed, left her hand and pointed at his reservation. "There you go." He smiled and straightened up, he thought I did not see but I did that he handed her his card that had his number and turned around.

I sighed and regretted coming here, he is *such* a flirt and I hate flirts. Asshole. I cursed in my brain.

Had I known what followed, I would have never accompanied him.

Chapter 5

Scarlette

We waited for the pre ordered food silently. I was in no mood of starting a conversation after what he did; I was just sitting in front of him and texting my cousin Alexandra Waters.

Alexandra- Hi sexy! Where are you?

Me- Date.

Alexandra- Bitch! You did not even tell me! Who is it? How is it going?

Me- Nothing great! With Jacob San Tiago.

Alexandra- Who????? Jacob heaven on Earth San Tiago from Groove!!!!!? Wait, you got a job there?

Me- Yup and yup!

Alexandra- Idiot! You are on a date with Jacob San Tiago and you are texting to Alexandra Waters. Insane or what? Be with him, he is sexy. Plzzz be sweet and kiss him ;)

Me- Alex! Really!

Alexandra- Not replying anymore! Be with him yeah? Btw have you told him about....?

Me- No Alex I have not and I will never. Until and unless I trust him.

Alexandra- Good! Okay bye now. You know I love you xx

"Scar?" Jacob made me look up, "Scarlette Waters. Yeah?" I replied coldly, "What are you mad at?" He asked. I rolled my eyes, "Like you care? Go become the receptionist's temporary fix!" I snapped.

"Jeaaloouuss??" He cooed, I gave him a disgusted face, "I *HATE* flirts." I eyed him intentionally; he shifted uncomfortably under my gaze.

"Excuse me?" The waiter came over, "Food for the handsome, young man and his beautiful lady. Lovely couple you both are." He greeted, even though I was mad but I could not help my cheeks turning a deep shade of crimson.

The waiter served the food, "The magical stars known as wine for the beautiful couple." He grinned and I smelled this as a pick up line from *The Fault In Our Stars by John Green*. My favorite book/movie.

"We are not a couple...yet." Jacob winked at me, yet! Yet! Yet? Are you going to ask me out, are you? Major Awwwww! I blushed again. The waiter, after serving, excused himself.

We had salad, extremely delicious gannnochi and wine that really tasted like stars. It was the best meal I *ever* had. The food covered up my anger on Jacob's flirting before.

After talking for a bit Jacob all of a sudden stood up, "Hello ladies and gentlemen! This girl in yellow is Scarlette Waters. My date for the evening and maybe even years to come. Can we all please sing a nice song for my crush?" He announced, I could really feel my insides screaming, heart pounding and eyes popping out.

Jacob had a *crush* on *me*.

He started belting out the lyrics of Teenage Dirtbag. It was so special and cute and adorable but...all this did not seem right; I was feeling so much anxiety. I don't know, I felt as if something was going to happen. Something wrong.

I was so busy thinking about all this that I did not notice Jacob had finished his song; I went over and hugged him while the others clapped. I sensed he wanted a kiss but I am not a girl to give up on such mild actions.

He pulled back licking his lips in a cute manner, "Thank you for this. I loved it." I smiled at him, he smiled back, he was about to lean in when my phone rang and I thanked God.

"Yeah mum?" I picked up the call, "Scarlette...there is a curfew in our area. Can you stay somewhere else dear?" She said in a small voice. I sighed, "Yeah mum. Bye. Love you." I replied, "Bye baby doll. Love you too. Take care." I smiled.

I looked at Jacob who had a full face smile on his face, "You will come to my place?" He wiggled his eyebrows; I shook my head, "Not alone with you." I clarified with a smirk.

"Who told you I live alone?" He chuckled, "I live with Shawn and Oliver. Abraham and Mark in another house." He consoled my restlessness a bit.

"Let us go." He smiled and let me in the car.

"Why do Mark and Abraham live in a different house?" I asked him, he shrugged casually, "Abraham likes to stay a bit alone, he is not that living with too many people kind of a person. He likes to have his alone time. Also because a house for five, with personal restrooms, a music room, living room, dining room and kitchen is usually not found. So we decided to split in three and two." He explained.

I nodded and looked out, London is beautiful, I thought with Love Story by Taylor Swift in the background.

Suddenly the car stopped, I turned to Jacob, and he was looking at me. I raised my eyebrows, "Uhm...C-can I kiss you Scarlette?" He took me by surprise.

I looked at him and saw a hint of innocence and hope written all over, I nodded and leaned in with my eyes closed. Our lips touched.

This kiss was meaningless; the taste of mint and his cologne lingered on to my lips. I felt nothing, it was *just* a kiss. No good, no bad. No romantic, no forced. It was of no meaning. It had no spark, no love, it was empty.

I pulled back breathlessly and bit my lip; he had a big smirk on his face. He bent and pecked my lips again, straightening; he set his hands on the steering wheel with a weird smirk now on his face.

Seeing that smirk I grew more and more nervous. I already was not feeling positive. This kiss and now this smirk, it made me more nervous.

I prayed the night to if, bring any changes and must be positive...

Chapter 6

Abraham

Isn't it a great thing when there is a pest control in your house hence you have to live with 4 people and sleep in the guest room? Yea, it is not and yea, this is my situation right now.

Ting Tong Ting

The doorbell rang, predicting it to be Shawn, who was out with his girlfriend Jennifer, I opened the door.

Scarlette

"C'mon Shaw-" Abraham, in a black shirt and blue jeans, opened the door but stopped as his eyes met mine, he was taken aback by my sudden appearance same as I was. He eyed me in amazement, "Scarlette!?" He looked at Jacob, "Jacob?" He raised his eyebrows.

"Curfew in her area. She needs a place to stay." He explained, "Why are you here?" It was now his turn to ask. Abraham seemed surprise, "Bro! I am here since the last 2 days. Pest control on at house." He replied a little shocked and I guess avoiding eye contact with me.

Jacob closed his eyes tightly, "Shit! I forgot." He mumbled, "I am so sorry babe. Want to come to a hotel?" He asked. "No. Guest room is empty. Plus, Shawn is out with Jennifer, Oliver has gone to visit his mum and Mark is asleep." Abraham interrupted. I eyed him.

He looked concerned, they both exchanged a few glances, and ultimately Abraham let us in with a confused expression while Jacob looked a bit angry. I decided against the decision of asking either of them anything.

"Want to come to my room for a little time? It's quite early I guess." Jacob turned and asked, I saw behind him Abraham cursing under his breath, and having no control on myself I nodded.

He took me into the room.

Abraham

I opened the door to see Jacob and the person I least expected to be here, Scarlette. I eyed her, she looked breathtaking in a yellow dress, and I must say she is one hell of a beautiful girl.

Jacob has a typical way ending dates- with sex. Yet he knows that I and Mark absolutely hate if he brings girls home for one night stands, that's why we bought a different house. Doing this is like cheating the innocent girls who look up to us as their idol and love us; it feels like deceiving our fans, deceiving our career and deceiving our families by questioning their upbringing. We hate this side of Jacob, the fuck boy Jacob.

I understood Jacob forgot about me and Mark sharing the house so he brought Scarlette home at least I saved her from causing trouble up in some hotel room with him that is, have sex, which I do not think she might be ready for. Here I can stop him if he tries to pursue her into doing something she is not ready for. However, before I could warn she already had agreed to spend time in his room.

Even though I was concerned for her yet I did not say anything and let her go.

I went into my room to continue with my drawings, being bored in their home as ever. I scattered all my colors and pages like I always do and started drawing random cartoons.

"Leave me Jacob! Jacob! Please Jacob leaaavveee!!" I heard Scarlette yell outside, I threw all the papers and colors kept on my lap and ran outside.

I opened the door of Jacob's room to find Scarlette leaned on the wall and Jacob on the top, trying to force himself. That time I could not save her, this time I will.

I went and held Jacob's shirt and pushed him away, Scarlette, unable to grasp the sudden happenings hugged me from one side. "Abraham!" She gasped for air.

"Abraham stay away!" Jacob yelled, "No I will *not* Jacob! I will not! You cannot do this with every girl and I cannot just let it happen! That is why I did not let her go to a hotel with you." I said and started to move out with Scarlette when I felt a strong hand on my shoulder.

I turned and looked at him dead in the eye, "Stay away or I will call Peter or even the media." I pointed, threatening him, his jaw tightened but he went away without a word.

I took her to my room, made her sit on the couch and ran back and brought water for her. I have seen Sarah like this, the situation of Scarlette gave me a kaleidoscope of memories. They just flashed like a movie in front of my eyes.

Scarlette looked exactly same as what Sarah was looking that night. The night things turned upside down, the night after what followed killed the old me.

Flashback

"Sarah!?" I yelled at what I saw. I ran to her, she was sitting on the couch, crying her eyes out.

Her white suit all crushed and crumpled her eyes red, cheeks drenched with tears and pain. Her makeup was entirely smudged up; her kohl was dripping, ruining her suit. She appeared so vulnerable and broken; I had never seen her that way before.

"Baby what's wrong? Please tell me." I kneeled down to her level, "Abraham I-I have to tell you something-"

End of flashback

I shook my thoughts away, went and sat next to her on the couch, "Have water Scarlette," I made her drink it myself; she was gasping for breath and hiccupping with tears never stopping.

She gulped the water down her throat with much pain, "It is okay Sara-Scarlette." I quickly corrected myself, "It is n-not okay A-Abraham. I was about to get raped. If you w-would not have not been here I..." she broke down again.

She looked up at me with gleaming eyes. Unable to understand what else to do I brought her to my embrace, I held her tight in my arms, as if she was a doll that would collapse any moment if I held her tighter. She sank her face into my chest as if to ask me to never let go as I put my arms around her.

We sat there in that way, finding a sense of safety in each other's arms, "It *is* okay Scarlette. I will never let you be misused by anyone. Trust me." I whispered to her and I think I felt her nod her head.

It was like we already knew each other, as we embraced with such intensity. Our arms around one another and chests pressed together, as warm tears continued to fall from her cheeks. Neither wanted to let go, but I had to. Slowly I pulled back; she still snuggled in me from one side. Her head was buried in my chest, her face all red and my shirt fabric was drenched in her tears. Seeing how sensitive and shocked she was with what just happened, I did not protest it. She reminded me so badly of Sarah.

"Can I go to the balcony with you Abraham? I need some air." She asked in a timid voice and I nodded. I made her stand up and opened the balcony door.

The cold breeze hit our faces, London was cold today. She held me like I was her anchor in a stormy sea.

I felt her having some difficulty; she was making sounds as if she was coughing. I made her face me, "Are you okay Scarlette?" I asked her.

Scarlette

"Are you okay Scarlette?" Abraham asked me as I struggled for breath due to my problem. I had to cry! Shit! I cannot show my ill side in front of him. "I n-need to…s-sit." I struggled for breath so hard…

He nodded and quickly made me sit on the hanging wooden chair at the corner near the railing, "Scarlette what happen? You look pale." He held my face in his hands in an insanely worried way.

I shook my head, casted my eyes on the floor and took 10-15 deep breaths. After taking breaths slowly for around 15 minutes I could become normal. I slowly looked up at Abraham who had confusion and concern written all over his face, "Are you okay?" He asked again.

"I am okay." I said slowly, clearly seeing that even though he was unconvinced he did not push it further. I stood up, went to the railing and leaned a bit on it, I tried to stop my tears but I could not. They just kept flowing out.

"Listen, it is all okay until and unless *you* are fine. You need to forget it okay?" Abraham came next to me and set his hand on mine. His words somehow convinced me that it is not a big deal, when he said that he would never let me misused, I instantly believed him. He had some kind of a magic on me. However that did not stop my heart from hammering against my ribs.

I faced him and hugged him, crying in his black fabric covered chest while my hands clung to his neck. He had bent a bit to reach till my height; his chin was resting on my shoulder, his arms holding me as if he would never let me go.

He made his arms feel like home.

Abraham

After being in each other's embrace till what felt as if forever, I pulled back and made her lean on my one shoulder. She yawned but quickly covered it up; I looked down at her and saw her eyes droopy, red and swollen from all the crying yet beautiful.

"Sleepy?" I asked her, she shook her head, "I will not sleep. He will come back. N-no." She said in a scared tone, I held her face and stroked her cheek with my thumb, "I will save you. I promise." I said and kissed her forehead, she nodded.

I took her to my room, laid her down and laid next to her, she closed her eyes. Being a bad actress, she pretended to sleep but her hands were shivering, I pulled her closer to me, intertwined our fingers and stroked her forehead to relax her.

I started to sing her my own song, the song that I had written to Sarah, to sleep,

"You were the light in my life

I've been searching for you all alone, yeah.

I was lost, you were the guide.

Taking me all the way along, all the way right.

I've never been the one who's going to love someone more, someone less, no.

I've never been the one to heal the scars of what you've done.

You're my healer, healer

But not the one

I can love and live with forever, ever

Believe me now

I just can't love you forever

If i let all my walls come down to crumble to the ground and tell you, yeah.

If i light up my past,

Would you still

Stay by me and cry with me ever, cry with me ever? Stay with me forever?

I've never been the one who's gonna love that, no.

I'll never be the one to shower my love.

You're my healer, healer but not the one

I can love and live with forever and ever.

Believe me now

I just can't love you forever, ever.

I say whatever it is, whatever it was

I cannot love you anymore.

I cannot love you for your good, for your happiness, I'll let you go.

You, my love, I just can't let you go but I have to let you go..."

I slowly ended the song and opened my eyes. I knew she had fallen asleep after the first paragraph but I needed to vent out my feelings to her. Whatever happens I am never going to tell her anything directly, I will not betray Sarah; I will be like I am, hidden behind this mask. I will not let her come close to me. I wanted her to listen closely to the songs I sung as the lyrics speak the words I fail to say.

I turned and saw her asleep, her hair falling on her face, making her look undeniably beautiful. Her face was flawless and attractive. Her sleeping face was so free from worries, anxieties, pain and fears. She looked so calmed down, not a soul would believe she was crying her heart out, minutes ago.

I got up slowly, not letting her wake up and covered her with a blanket, turned on the air-conditioner and stroked my hand on her forehead, kissing it slowly, I went to the couch.

I heard some faint ringing sound from the living room; I went out to see a phone ringing the belonged neither to me, Jacob nor Mark.

The caller ID flashed, *"Ellie"* with a picture of a girl looking quite similar to Scarlette. I understood that it was Scarlette's phone.

I picked up the call, "Scarlette where are you? I have been calling you since ages! Mum thinks we have had a talk. You know, I was so worried!" A shrill female voice shouted the minute I pressed the 'accept call' button, "Um, I am sorry. She is sleeping." I replied, "Who are you?" She asked, confused.

"I am Abraham...Abraham Khan, Scarlette's um... *friend.*" I was not quite comfortable calling her my friend after one meeting and also after deciding to not let her come close to me.

"Oh I am sorry; I thought she got into some trouble. Sorry! By the way I am Ellie Waters, Scarlette's younger sister. When she gets up tell her Ellie had called." She grew normal.

"Any messages?" I asked, "Yeah tell her to hav - uh, no no. Uh, no messages. Just ask her to call me when she gets up. Thank you so much." She quickly covered up something she was about to say but I did not push it, personal matter maybe.

"Yeah okay. You are welcome. Bye." I disconnected the call and went back to the room.

Taking a cushion and quilt I lay down on the couch in front of the bed and rewind today's events in my head.

Deciding never to tell Scarlette anything, not betraying Sarah and thinking of her, I drifted off to sleep.

Unknown to the fact that I was not the one writing my life but God is.

Chapter 7

<u>Scarlette</u>

I woke up with the sun pierce my eyes, not able to recognize the surroundings I jumped out of the bed and landed on the floor.

I slowly realized that the entire night I had spent here in Abraham's bed; just yesterday there was an attempt to rape me and Abraham was the one who had helped me out. I checked my clothes; thankfully there was no second attempt.

I freaked out when I did not see him around. He was nowhere in my sight, I so wanted him to be with me. Not staring at me sleep all night like a creep/vampire or like Christian Grey from *Fifty Shades of Grey* or Edward Cullen from *Twilight* but he should have been in the room.

Due to headache I did not want to leave the room as yet; my head was bursting. For all I knew either Jacob was there and stood right outside the bedroom door, waiting for me, to take revenge or I was here with Abraham, safe and sound.

Somehow my mind made me believe that I was safe because Abraham was there, with me, for me. I knew what I was thinking was right but he was a different soul, my subconscious reminded me. He can flip *anytime*, come on he is Abraham Khan!

He did not want me to be after completing the While We Are tour in the morning and few hours later he promised to save me always and sung me to sleep at night.

Not a minute later after being in deep thought, I knew something was right. Something with him, something with me and something with us.

The longer I waited, the lesser opportunity I had to save myself just in case, Abraham was not there and I was in real danger. Otherwise, I would go, thank him and go back to my house as quick as possible.

Still half asleep, I grabbed my phone that had battery dead, paced around the bedroom contemplating if I should walk out or not, and finally, decided to take the leap of faith and open his room's door.

Before I took a step out of the door I checked the clock: 8:30am it said. I woke up late, had to join office today at 10:00am and here I was, lying in someone's bed whom I met just yesterday.

I turned back and saw a quilt and pillow on the couch in front I smiled. What a gentleman this guy is! I quietly went out.

"Abraham," I said slowly as I went out searching for him, "Good morning Scarlette." A voice came from the kitchen, without any enthusiasm. I went to the direction and saw all of the boys and their girlfriends (probably) smiling at me. Shoot! I did not even make my hair while all of them were well dressed.

"M-morning." I forced a smile without making any eye contact with Jacob who was piercing my body with his stare. Seeing me, Abraham came out of the kitchen, "Take." He handed me a cup of coffee, I smiled at him but he turned back.

I am always right, he flipped. I sipped the coffee, "Hi I am Jennifer Cullen. Shawn's girlfriend and Victoria Secret's model." A beautiful girl got up and shook hands with me, intimidating me by her looks. She looked gorgeous in a white shirt and blue denim jeans and here I was, looking like a wild animal, in a yellow Coco Chanel dress at 8:30 in the morning and hair flying in all directions.

"Hello I am Scarlette Waters. Their new stylist." I replied with the warmest smile, I could give, with a throbbing head.

"How are you here?" She asked curiously, pulling her hand back. "Actually I went out with uh, um, Jacob. Curfew hit my area and I had no place to spend the night so... I stayed here." I explained her. She tried to stifle her smile, I raised my eyebrows and she nodded in a 'wait I will explain' way.

"You uhm, went out with *Jacob* and came out of *Abraham's* room? And wait, you spent a night in *the Abraham Khan*'s room?" She said surprisingly.

Before I could reply she turned to Abraham, "Abraham boi you never let me *sit* in your room for more than an hour. And you let her all night without uhm... *any*thing. How *sweet* of you?" She said sarcastically.

"Jennifer you cannot let a girl be alone if she is in an unsafe place." He said eyeing Jacob. In order to avoid any more questions from a confused Jennifer he looked at me, "Scarlette you go take a shower and get a pair of clothes from Jessica. Get ready and we will drop you home." He said plainly, without even asking me how I was.

I nodded and went to the room. "How weird he is." I mumbled collecting my things. "Uhm Scarlette?" A female voice called me that my mind registered was not Jennifer's.

I turned back to see a pretty girl with straight hair in a black sleeveless balloon top and white jeans. She had some clothes in her hands and I guessed her to be Jessica.

"Hi...Jessica?" I said a questioning tone and she nodded with a grin. "Hi I am Jessica Smith, Oliver's girlfriend and a Coco Chanel model. Ah Abraham asked me to give you these clothes." She said handing me the clothes she was holding, "And uhm I know what happened last night. I am *so* sorry for that.» She apologized as if it was her fault.

"It's okay. Why are you sorry? And by the way all of you know? Like, Jennifer was laughing outside so..." I stopped for her to speak.

"No no. Oliver is Jacob's best friend, he told Oliver about the fight and I know just because I am his girlfriend rest everyone is clueless. It won't be safe for Jacob. He has already tarnished one *and* the band's reputation. Jennifer is chirpy and crazy do not take things she says to heart. Actually, Abraham *never* like *ever* lets anyone into his room for more than an hour even if it is a matter of death and life. He is a bit selfish and possessive regarding his things. You were in for *one full night* without doing anything. You know what I mean right?" She asked and I nodded knowing she was talking about sex.

"So yeah, that was what she was saying. Do not take it the other way." She smiled.

"Anyways, I want to ask you this ever since you came out. Can I?" She asked. I nodded with raised eyebrows. "Great. Uh that is a Coco Chanel dress right?" She asked with a delighted expression and I nodded with a chuckle.

"This dress is from the vintage period, very unique and very beautiful. It is absolutely beautiful." She complimented the dress. "Thank you Jessica and if you want to wear it anytime you can surely take it!" I grinned.

"Sure?" She asked and I nodded slowly feeling a kind of bond forming between us. "Oh and by the way, thank you for these," I said motioning to the clothes, "I will return y-" she shook her head.

"This is a rule regarding the Groove girls...we do not return things to each other that we take. That is how you become girl friends no?" She said with a slight pat on my shoulder and left the room. *Such* a sweetheart!

I saw the clothes, it was a white crop top and maroon leggings. Even though I was insecure with my body being the crop top type yet I decided to wear it anyways. Hah! As if I had any options.

I turned back hearing an alarm ring that was maybe Abraham's, I shut it off after a mental battle of touching his things or not. "I am sorry Scarlette." I heard a slow and slurry voice call me from behind, a voice that made a chill run down my spine and body shiver with memories flashing back.

I gulped hard turning back, "J-Jacob." This was all I could. "I am sorry Scar. I am really very sorry, I thought you too...you too had fallen for me. When I saw you I had this love at first sight kind of feeling. After the kiss I thought you too..." he sighed, "I am sorry Scarlette." He said with innocence dripping from his face.

I could not manage to ditch him with those puppy dog eyes, I took a deep breath, "It is okay. Do not do this again." I said and turned back.

"I promise." He mumbled and I heard footsteps leave the room. I just wish he keeps promises.

Without any other thoughts I went in for a shower.

Abraham

I do not want Scarlette to be close to me so I am acting harsh even though it is killing me inside. I felt so magical last night, holding her in my arms, it felt natural. God knows how I was stopping myself from kissing her yesterday; my will power is something to appreciate.

However natural or beautiful it felt to have Scarlette with me I will not be with her. I will not forget Sarah Zaidi, my valentine forever. I lost her due to myself, I am the one to be blamed and now this is my way of compensating for that.

It did not go in my head why had I shown my *actual* and sensitive side to Scarlette last night, the person in me, which was behind the wall of arrogance I had put in front to keep people away from me. The side that had feelings, resting in the deepest pits.

I looked up in the mirror hanged above the door that reflects sunlight in the entire room to bring pureness. (Jessica and her logics only God and she herself can understand.)

Anyways, I saw Scarlette's reflection; she had an utterly confused and lost expression on her face as she stared at me.

I raised my eyebrows, "Hi." She said quickly covering her confusion with a smile as I eyed her turning back. She looked kind of sexy in a white crop top complimenting her physique, maroon leggings and hair falling down freely.

"Hi. Come have breakfast then we will drop you home." I said plainly to her and turned to the kitchen, "I will serve her Abraham you go." Jessica smiled at me as she set Scarlette's plate; I nodded and went for a shower.

Scarlette

To avoid sitting there and feeling awkward while Jessica cooked I went and started helping her.

"You need not help it is okay!" She said quickly as she saw me doing the dishes. "It is okay Jessica. I felt super awkward sitting there while you work here." She chuckled.

"Uhm Jessica, can I ask you something?" I asked her slowly, she looked up, "Firstly, call me Jess, everyone does, I mean all my friends. Jessica sounds formal and yeah, go on." She flashed her smile and continued her work. "Who is Sarah?" I asked her, she looked up with a confused look on her face, "Err...Who is Sarah? I do not think...No; I do not know any Sarah. Where did you hear about this girl?" She asked curiously.

"Just now when Abraham was standing in front of that mirror he mumbled, 'No Abraham shut up, no Scarlette. Only Sarah.' And because he mentioned me so I am hella curious to know." I explained to her. She nodded a bit, "Sorry Scar, I hope I can call you that but even if you do not allow me I will. But anyways, sorry but I do not know this Sarah girl." She made a disappointed face and I just nodded with a shrug.

After enjoying a delicious treat of sandwiches and juice I got up to leave. My head was still throbbing from all the crying last night. I bid them adieu and waved plainly to Jacob with an extremely fake smile.

In the car

"Ready?" Abraham asked putting the car in ignition and I nodded in reply. I was still confused to why did he say those words, there was definitely something related to that girl and maybe to me also.

Who was Sarah? How is she related to him? Where is she? Such questions floated in my brain but I did not ask him anything. We weren't that close yet and never will be.

"Thank you so much for last night." I said looking down, "It is okay. You are welcome." He said plainly.

"What is up with your tone since morning?" I asked unable to keep it in my head anymore, "I am like this only." He said without even glancing at me.

"Okay. So what *was* up with you last night?» I asked him with raised eyebrows, his expression seemed to stiffen, «Where is your house?» He avoided my question.

"I do not know." I replied, he frowned and stopped the car, "What is your problem Scarlette?" He seemed irritated. "If you do not answer to what I am asking I will also *not* answer your question!" I replied back with a smile and folded arms.

He groaned, "What on Earth do you want to know?" He cried.

"Why do you flip? You were a sugar pudding last night, ready to save me against all odds and now you are salt less food. What is up with you and your flips?" I said in an irritated tone.

His eyes darkened and he took a deep breath.

"I am like this only. I have uhm sisters b-back home; I know what it feels like if there are questions raised on a girl's character. So I p-protected you." He seemed lost and sad as he spoke about his sisters.

"Oh uhm okay. Anyways, thank you." I flashed a grin and he just nodded in response.

"Now where is your house?" Abraham asked in an irritated way, I smiled a bit, "Amen Street. House no. 12." I told him, he thought a bit before nodding.

"Uhm this is for you." He said after a while hesitantly, licking his lips while handing me a plastic bag.

"What is this?" I asked taking them from him. He cleared his throat, "Uh t-these are medicines. You slept crying last night. You might be having a headache." He said so nervously as if he was asking me for marriage.

I smiled, "Thank you so much. I am having bomb blasts in my head." I said opening the knot. I took out the yellow and red medicines.

Which one was for what? I looked at them, confused.

Ask Abraham my one part said.

Google it my second part said.

Suddenly Abraham said something, "Sorry? What?" I asked, startled, as I could not hear him. "Uh the red one is for headache and yellow for fever. Just in case." He smiled faintly handing me his water bottle.

I smiled taking it from him and swallowed the medicine. It was awful.

Abraham

Scarlette swallowed the medicine with much difficulty and made a bad face, not bad actually but she looked insanely cute like that.

She had crinkled up her nose and eyes, her lips made a small pout and her eyes were closed.

I could not help the chuckle escaping my lips; she turned to me with questioning eyes.

"Uhm you looked adorable with that expression on." I blabbered as if some magical power made me do it.

She widened her eyes, looking cuter, "Abraham Khan complementing someone. I wish I could record this." She said sarcastically, "Oh and thank you again." She said with an eye blink and smile.

I continued driving with literally tying my brain so that I did not say anything or just crash my lips with hers.

"That is my house." She said pointing towards a small house; it was nothing big or showy. It reminded me of my own house back home at Bradford.

Her house brought back to me many memories that were supposed to be buried deep inside.

I stopped the car in front of it.

Scarlette

Abraham stopped the car in front of my house; I turned to him and smiled.

I took him by surprise as I hugged him. Not tightly or anything but just a friendly one, the one that I wanted badly. I expected him to put me away but instead he rested his chin on my head and rubbed my back.

I felt myself giving up in his warm embrace, "Thank you so much for everything Abraham." My voice sounded muffled in his chest.

We were of perfect height difference, our headline was perfect. While wrapped in his arms, the warmth was not what urged me to stay like that but because I could hear his heartbeat. Slow and steady.

"It's okay. You're welcome Scarlette." He whispered and took me by surprise by kissing my head.

Realizing our awkward situation now, I pulled back and smiled faintly at him and got the same in reply.

I turned over and got out of the passenger door, the cold air hit my face hard; I regretted wearing a crop top and rubbed my arms. Hearing another door open and close I turned to see him coming out of the car.

He came to me, holding something in his hands. "Wear it first." He handed me a *'Nirvana' zipper* hoodie that I guess was men's. "No it's okay. I w-will m-manage." I said while shivering a bit.

"Manage to speak properly first. Now wear this and go or you will have to skip work due to illness. That will not make Peter very happy!" He said in an 'as a matter of fact' tone.

I wore it and zipped it up, "I will return you once I-" He raised his hands to stop me. "Keep it. It will help you out." He said motioning his hand, and I just shrugged.

The hoodie had his smell, the smell of his musk perfume I had smelled yesterday. It also had a hint of ash in it and I guessed that he had smoked while wearing this.

I thanked him and turned to walk off, I turned back again to expect an empty road but saw him in the same position. Leaning on the car, with crossed hands and looking at me.

"Go." I told him, he shook his head. "You go first." He insisted and I turned to walk over again.

As I reached and rang the bell the door was opened by Ellie who was too sleepy to talk. She smiled at me and turned away to her room, scratching her head. I got in and turned to him, he still stood there. I waved to him and he waved back with a small smile.

I quickly closed the door and ran to the window. Peeping through one side I saw him standing straight and go to the driver seat.

Chapter 8

<u>Scarlette</u>

"MUM! I'M HOME!" I yelled turning from the window to find her standing behind with crossed arms.

"Morning." I said with a smile. "Who dropped you home?" She questioned me sternly.

"Ahm...a...friend!" I dodged her question and turned to the stairs. "I have never seen you wearing a hoodie. That too Nirvana!" She asked me from behind as I climbed two stairs. "It's freezing outside! It's better to wear a Nirvana hoodie than sneeze for the whole week." That's right I hate Nirvana.

"So Abraham Khan likes Nirvana?" I quickly faced her and saw her with crossed her arms. I quickly covered the hoodie with my hands, "Who is Abraham Khan?" I asked innocently, she gave me a 'what did you just say?' kind of look.

As soon as I realized what she was thinking, I wanted to make an entire arena applaud for my amazing brain. I went on a date with Jacob San Tiago and did not know who Abraham Khan was. Okay. How intelligent can I be? *Gives standing ovation to self*

"I saw him outside. By the way you suck at lying." She said simply as if it was just a normal and daily thing. "Yeah okay. Abraham dropped me home and this is his hoodie and I stayed at the Jacob's house all night without doing anything like having sex. Shit sorry!" I shrugged and she widened her eyes at the choice of my words.

"And you did not take medicines and that tattoo boy has a crush on you." She gave me a toothy grin and I just gave her a confused face. "Really mum? Abraham Yaser Khan has a crush on me? Phu-leez! He is a part of the biggest boy band and has a billion, no, a million girls after him that are much skinnier and sexier than me. Why will he crush over a girl he met yesterday if he has a girl like Selena Gomez as his friend?" I stated my facts.

Okay, I thought Jacob had a crush on me but now I know he did that only to take me to his bed. He does not crush over me and is only a fuckboy.

"Scarlette looks are not always everything. Maybe he found you simple and sweet." She shrugged, I just rolled my eyes. "And why do you think that?" I asked her.

"Come on, he dropped you home; you were with him all night and have returned back without *doing* anything, you know. He gave you his hoodie and did not leave until you were in the house." She spoke while counting on her fingers.

"Done mum?" I asked her crossing my arms.

"Scarlette please do not tell him anything about your di-" here she goes on and on about my disease.

"Enough mum! Enough! Thank you for making me realize that I'm a failed experiment hundred times a day and not helping me move on, by just going on and on about this heck idiotic disease. I pretend to be happy all the time but you bring this up every time and bring my confidence level from zenith to nadir. Knowing that I will die one day, that will be too soon, is scary. Guess what? News flash: NO ONE GIVES A SHIT! Whether I die or I live! Abraham is not going to do *anything* even if I tell him okay? He just does not care! Now shut up!» I yelled at the top of my voice, irritated and angry about hearing the same thing thousand times a day.

I looked up at mum to say sorry, teary eyed but saw her staring wide eyed at something behind me. I knitted my eyebrows together and turned back.

"Abraham!" I stared at him who was staring back at me with shock and confusion written all over his face.

"Uh S-Scarlette you left your dress. In the car." He handed me my bag and looked down. "Uh, um, I-Thank you." I said in my mouth.

"Since when are you standing here? And when did you come in?" I wiped my eyes

"Uh I-when you said h-he just does not care and uh yeah." He looked down. All three of us knew he was lying and had heard every word that left my mouth.

Abraham

Okay now I am confused. This girl is so mysterious. She is so normal like this but this disease thing had made her mad. Her mum, I and she all knew I was lying but she did not push it further.

I heard every single word she said. Moving on? Disease? Death? Me not caring? What was she talking about?

"Uhm you must be Abraham Khan?" Her mum peeked from behind her. "Yeah." I replied. "You are shivering son. Uh Scarlette take him to your room I will get you both coffee." She beamed at us.

We both turned to each other, "Uh mum ac-" Scarlette was quieted by her mum's hand. "Some other day for sure." I smiled at her, she shook her head, "You brought my daughter home safe. It's a token of thank you from my side." She said and turned away to the kitchen.

"Seems like we do not have an option." I turned to her and shrugged, she sighed and nodded. "Come." She motioned and I followed her.

She quietly opened the door of her room. I followed her and we entered into an extremely dirty room. It seemed like a tornado had just hit the place.

Scarlette

I opened the door of my room and immediately regretted it. God! While changing for the date yesterday I never realized I left the room looking like nothing but a garbage bin. My clothes make up stuff and accessories were all around the room.

"Your bedroom is a mess." Abraham chuckled as he entered into the room behind me. "You should see my life." I whispered to myself with a chuckle.

"Sorry, did you say something?" He turned to me with raised eyebrows and innocent expression. I gave a fake confused face, "Um no." He looked at me making me shift uncomfortably under his gaze, "I can hear nicely but you cannot lie nicely. That is a fact." He told me indirectly that he had heard what I had spoken.

He stared at me with those deep, brown eyes and the stares burned into my skin. I avoided his eyes and picked up the clothes scattered on the bed and kept them in the wardrobe to make space for us to sit down. He sat down on the bed while looking around the room and I sat on the chair next to it. We sat awkwardly looking everywhere but each other.

"I do care Scarlette." He broke the silence looking at me and I was not thankful for it. "Uhm, sorry?" I raised my eyebrows at him. "I do care if something happens to you." He looked down and left me in a state of shock.

"The Abraham Khan" cares about me. The rude, bitchy and snobby Khan cares about me. What is wrong with him? He was behaving like a girl on periods- He was having major mood swings.

One minute he did not want me after tour, second minute he promised to protect me forever, third minute he avoided me at the Jacob's house, fourth minute he gave me medicines and dropped me home safely and now he cares.

Okay, what is seriously wrong with Abraham?

Seeing no reply from me he looked up at me with eyes as dark as a full moon night sky. "You can share things with me if you want. I *will* listen." He said in a reassuring way and I just sighed. "I have a past, Abraham. Something that I do not want to share with anyone." I blurted out and immediately regretted it.

"Same story here Scarlette." He said with a chuckle, as if mocking himself and looked down again.

Chapter 9

A week later

"Scarlette the boys are going for an interview tomorrow. The outfits are ready?" Anne Cordo, their hair stylist, a lady with hair of multiple colors, asked me as she entered my small styling room.

"Yes Anne. Only the sizes have to be checked, if you can please send the boys?" I pleaded her innocently knowing it was a difficult task. It is easier to tame a hungry dog than putting the Groove lads into one room once they are up to their naughtiness i.e. 24/7.

"That is a tough job, but…okay, that is my job." She chuckled and excused herself to call the boys who were busy in so called "perfecting" their dance.

The entire world knows how horrible Groove is when it comes to dancing! They basically take the piss out of the most weird, easy and uncoordinated dance moves but because they dance with confusion and cuteness all over their faces so fans don't complain but appreciate their efforts.

In short, Groove boys are the worst dancers you will come across but because of their adorable mistakes you will not mind the dance.

"Sa-car-lette!!" Shawn yelled as all the five boys barged into the room one by one and squeezed them, on a small couch. "Shawn! Why do you keep yelling all the time?" I asked him as I was petrified because of the sudden yelling.

All of them looked hell different than what they look at stage. Jacob was wearing a loose, white t-shirt with black shorts. Abraham was wearing a loose, black vest that had weird black designs on it paired with black pants. Shawn paired his black and white adidas gym outfit. Oliver wore a grey t-shirt and blue shorts. Mark looked cute in a black t-shirt and black shorts.

"Because I louve you!" Shawn said, intentionally saying 'love' as 'louve' knowing I dislike the way it sounds. I rolled my eyes at him, "Of course you do." I said sarcastically.

"Ow!" Suddenly Jacob yelled making all of us turn to him.

"Err...Sorry." He said sheepishly, "What is up?" Oliver asked with concern. "Mark hit me on my broken arm." He said, glaring at Mark who was laughing his ass off.

On the concert yesterday Jacob fell down on the stage while trying to save Oliver from falling off into a crowd of hungry fans. Had Shawn not spilled water on the entire stage, Jacob would have had an unbroken arm. The matter of shock was that Mark and Abraham were eating chips when Jacob fell and both of them laughed instead of picking him up. TRUE FRIENDSHIP IS PROTECTION- Lol yeah!

"Mark...shh!" I tried to make him quite but he continued laughing. I mentally face palmed- Once when Mark Merchant starts laughing there is no end.

"Anyways, you guys have an interview tomorrow," Shawn interrupted me, "Thanks for the news Scar!" He said sarcastically with a smirk dancing on his face.

I rolled my eyes at him, "So check that your outfits fit you properly yeah?" I asked them and they nodded obediently in reply. "Good boys."

I smiled and turned around to get their packets.

I picked up the five packets and turned back to see the five boys standing in front of their respective mirrors.

"Marker." I read and knitted my eyebrows, I remember the slip I had put on the packets had their full names and this was not my handwriting but a very messy one.

I understood who did it and looked up at Shawn, "Care to explain?"

I crossed my arms on my chest.

He grinned goofily, "Those were too perfect to handle you know!" the others laughed, face palmed and I could not help but laugh at his immaturity.

Who will guess that he was the oldest in the band yet the naughtiest of all?

"Moving on, Mark there you go." I said shaking my head with a smile and threw Mark's packet that he catches easily. He went off to change and I picked up the next one.

"Spoon lover." I read and knew who it was for, Oliver; he had a phobia of spoons and gets teased a hundred times about it by Shawn.

Oliver looked up at me with a surprised face and I turned the label towards him, "Talk to Shawn about it. I wrote Oliver J Edwards." I gave him a small smile and he took the packet after glaring at Shawn.

"Swag Master Shawn." I chuckled and sighed at the same time; he walked to me with swag and took the packet, "I know you still love me." He grinned and I nodded, "Who can hate the shade master?" He laughed and went back to where he stood instead of going to change.

"Scarlette lover." I blurted out but realized quickly and looked at Shawn wide eyed.

"Uh I mean…Jacob." He gave another goofy grin; I looked towards Jacob who looked down as his eyes met mine, from the corner of my eyes I could see Abraham frowning at Shawn.

"Uh okay, whatever." I said and handed the packet to Jacob who did not dare to look at me but quietly walked away while dragging Shawn with him.

I shook my head at this stupidity and took out the last packet.

I knew last packet was obviously Abraham's but read it to see Shawn's creativity. "Bradford Rebel."

I said and looked at Abraham who was staring wide eyed at the floor while I had a hard time stifling my laughter.

He was given this name when he first came into the band because he was a badass, a teenager, hailed from Bradford and thought it was cool, but now he dislikes it greatly.

"Uh Abraham...there you go." I pretended to look serious but by the look on his face I knew I was failing miserably. "It is okay, you can laugh. Shawn is stupid...and so is this name." He shook his head and took the packet while I laughed a little.

"No, it is actually really nice." I smiled and shrugged, he looked up, "You think so?" He asked innocently. I nodded, "Yeah, it is nice." He chuckled, "Might be." He smiled and went off to change. I turned back to remove the plastic bag.

"Scarlette!" After a few minutes, I heard Shawn yell and I turned back, startled yet rolling my eyes.

"Again shou-" I paused and eyed each one of them from head to toe, they actually looked really good. All of them wore brown t-shirts and black shoes with black jeans accompanied with a black coat, except Mark.

"You guys look good!" I exclaimed. "We are Groove, we always look good!" Oliver winked at me. "Except-" Mark interrupted, "Jacob's coat." He said and all turned to Jacob whose coat was upside down.

"No, um, it is...fine." He smiled a little at me. "No it is not Jacob; you have worn it upside down that is why it looks weird." I went to him. I took off his coat and straightened it, "There you go." I handed him his coat.

"I cannot wear it myself with a broken arm. Shawn helped me out." Jacob said in a confusedly innocent manner, "Uh okay, wait I will help you." I said and walked up to him because I had already walked back to my table.

"Is it hurting?" I asked him as I carefully was making him wear the coat. He did not reply but kept looking at me, "Jacob? Is it hurting?" I asked him again.

"With you around, all the pain goes away." He spoke making me look up at him, to confirm his words. We looked into each other's eyes with gazes locked for what seemed like ages. I just looked at him and he looked back at me, not caring about who was around.

Suddenly someone cleared their throat startling both of us and breaking our eye contact; I turned to look at Abraham, who had cleared his throat, now had anger on his face. "Uh, I, we-never mind." I tried to explain myself but failed in doing so.

He eyed first me and then Jacob, tightening his jaw he took off the coat, threw it on the couch and stormed out of the room. "Abraham!" I yelled and tried to stop him and went behind him.

All of a sudden a strong hand held my elbow, "Let him go." Jacob spoke, I turned to him, "No, I cannot. You just stay out of this." I snapped making him leave my elbow. "Ooooh jealous! Looks like I need to give Jacob's name to someone else." Shawn mumbled I glared at him before going behind Abraham.

I looked everywhere but could not find him. "May!" I called to a girl with pink hair, my assistant and Shawn's sister. "Yes Scarlette." She stopped, "Saw Abraham?" I asked hurriedly. "Uh…Yeah, he's in the field." She pointed at the door. I smiled and nodded at her before going to the field.

He stood there, leather jacket on and cigarette in his hand as he stood a few meters away with his eyes on the trees in front of him. His other hand was balled into a fist, making me realize he was angry.

"Abraham!" I say aloud, he spun right around in surprise. He looked at me and opened his mouth to blow out smoke, and just waited, his eyes dark and jaw tightened.

Seeing the burning cigarette in his hand, I hesitated a bit, knowing my condition. But, taking the huge leap of faith, I stepped forward.

"What is up with you? Why did you leave and just storm out like this?" I asked him, he took a long drag and blew it out. I felt the smoke go through my nose and enter my lungs, making it slightly difficult for me to talk.

"You guys were behaving like cheese balls. Romancing and throwing cheesy, SRK dialogues." He spoke with irritation clear in his voice. "Who is SRK?" I asked him in a confused manner.

He thought for a bit and face palmed, "You do not know him I guess. He is an Indian superstar. The king of romance in India. Jacob was behaving like him and so were you! I so wanted to play a romantic song in the background." He spoke with sass, clearing my confusion.

"Sorry…I got carried away." I confessed, looking down, "You got *carried away*?" He spitted.

Wait, why was he behaving like my boyfriend? Is he…*jealous*? Duh, no, I am not the type of girl that can woo Abraham Khan.

I just looked down, "Scarlette, Jacob's not good for you. The last time you were with him he tried to take advantage of you. Had you been in a hotel God knows what he would have done! Please Scarlette understand what I am saying." He said holding my shoulders.

I looked up at him and he quickly removed his hands. Just as he was about to take another drag, I held his hand, "Not right now, I-I am…allergic to the smell of ash." I lied with utter confidence. "Huh. Fine." He snorted and threw it down before crushing it under his foot.

"Please come in, everyone is in there, we need to see how the outfits look. I will be fired if you guys look bad. Though you will not, like obviously, but anyways, please?" I slowly pleaded with a puppy dog face and innocent eyes; he looked at me, thought for a bit before nodding and walking ahead.

"Why do you care for me Abraham?" I asked him suddenly, not that I intended to say that but it just flew out. I quickly regretted it within a fraction of seconds as he turned to face me with sort of a sad and lost face.

"Wh-why do I care for you? Uh…Because…" he gulped hard, "Hey! You are not some special museum statue okay? I respect and care for all the girls. Be it you or May or Anne or any other crew girl. I told you, I have tons of sisters. I do not let the crew girls much around Jacob, knowing what kind of a person he is. I even stop the fans at times, do not be so self-centered!" He said in a harsh tone.

Ouch. Okay, his words had cut me deeper than a knife, they hurt.

I nodded and controlled my tears while walking away, soon I felt a strong hand hold my bicep and pull me. "Abraham what are you doing?" I asked, trying to free myself from his grip, yet it was a fact I was a tiny not so strong fellow while he was a 5 ft 10 inches tall boy with biceps and abs.

"Scarlette…" His voice had a surprising calmness in it; it was a sweet and angelic sound. My name had never sounded so good, "I lied. I do care about you…a lot. It will kill me to see you heartbroken by a dork like him." He whispered in my ear before leaving a kiss on my left cheek and walking away while leaving me to blush with a big grin on my face replacing my tears.

After spending a good five minutes trying to absorb what happened I hid my grin with a normal smile and walked back to my room where the boys stood in their outfits.

Chapter 10

<u>Abraham</u>

We were going to the 'Night Talk Show', the biggest show in the United Kingdom, for the first time. Sitting in the green room, I was hell scared, not scared really but nervous. "Lads, are we ready?" Oliver asked with a lot of uncertainty.

We looked at each other with doubtful eyes, "Yeah, okay. We have to do this." Mark spoke as if finally gathering courage and all of us nodded. We put our right hands over one another's, "3...2...1...We go." All of us spoke our pump up line together.

A knock on the door interrupted us, "Who is it?" I asked loudly. "Uh it is me, Scarlette." She spoke, even if she had not taken her name, I would have recognized her voice. "Yeah, come in." I replied.

She wore a white 'Girls are sassy' sleeveless t-shirt, denim shorts, white converse with hair in a loose ponytail. When she had come in the morning she was wearing some sort of a blue long coat that was covering her body till her knees but took it off because it grew hot.

"Hi boys!" she chirped in her usual loud manner, "Hi." Shawn replied in a low voice. "Shawn William Cordan is quite today? Weird." She looked around and her eyes met mine, "Who died?" She asked me with raised eyebrows. By now I have understood that she loves to raise her eyebrows and roll her eyes.

I gave a confused look in reply.

"Why are all of you guys moving around with a constipated cum upset face huh?" She raised her eyebrows again as she looked at everyone. "They're tensed." Anne announced as she appeared behind Oliver, "Going to the first time on *such* a popular show so they are hell nervous." She explained.

"Oh come on you guys! You are Groove! The most popular, talented, handsome and awesome boy band in the world. You people are born confident and perfect!" Scarlette grinned at us.

"Nobody is perfect." I said, looking down, "Trust me...you are perfect." She replied in a voice that had faith in it, like she meant what she said. I looked up and saw her already looking at me, as soon as our eyes met; she looked away while I smiled to myself.

"Guys, you must go on the stage now, it is time for the show to start." May announced as she entered the room, making the adrenaline rush in us. I looked for my phone in my coat, but did not find it.

"All the best." Scarlette came over and spoke to me. I ignored her as I was in a tensed state, I always look at Sarah's picture but I could not find my phone today. "Abraham?" She asked again this time.

I looked up at Scarlette and saw that she had changed into the blue coat she wore in the morning, it was of the same type like the one I had gifted Sarah once, I stared at her and somehow found Sarah in her.

My Sarah, my lucky charm, my Scarlette.

Instead of looking for my phone for Sarah's picture I smiled at Scarlette, "Thank you." I hugged her, at first she was taken aback but soon she chuckled and hugged me back. After pulling back, she went over and hugged the others except Jacob whom she just wished with a small smile.

We left the green room and went to the stage when Sharlie Monis, the host of the 'Night Talk Show' announced, "Give it up for Groove!" The words had not flown out from her mouth that the entire audience clapped.

I looked towards the crowd and the adrenaline kicked in me but I saw something or rather someone in the first row that comforted me with their big, brown eyes…Scarlette. She had a big smile on her face, "All the best, you will rock." She mouthed to me with raised thumbs and I gave her a small smile in reply.

"Hello guys, please make yourself; comfortable." We hugged Sharlie one by one and sat on the gigantic couch that was kept for us, gigantic because we are five dudes and a small couch makes one of us sit on the floor. "How is it being here Abraham?" She asked me with a warm smile.

My hands started sweating as soon as she shot the question at me; I gulped hard, "It is absolutely great, like, pure magic. It is lovely to see all our fans here and you, obviously. We are really massively grateful to all the Groovers for their never ending support and love that has brought us in such a big show and made us so popular in just 3 years. To everyone," I turned to the crowd, "You are perfect." I said looking into Scarlette's eyes.

She seemed slightly surprised by my gesture, she blinked her eyes a number of time, looked at the ground and I guess I saw her cheeks turn in to a deep shade of crimson.

"Who all are taken?" Sharlie asked and everyone except me and Jacob raised their hands while we laughed and high fived one another. It is not that we are enemies, Jacob is a sweet and trustworthy friend but when it comes to girls he becomes a fuck boy and I absolutely hate that version of him.

"Jacob you are single and so are you Abraham?" She questioned us and we nodded with pouted lips, "Jacob?" She questioned with shock evident in her voice. "I *am* single but I am seeing someone at the time. I mean, I like her but she does not know." He said looking at the crowd, revealing his dimples.

All five of us knew whom he was talking about, Scarlette John Waters.

"Can we know who the lucky lady is?" She asked with a grin while the crowd yelled and from the corner of my eyes I could see Scarlette staring wide eyed at Jacob. "Uhm…I don't think so." He shook his head, a sigh of relief went through me and I guess Scarlette too. "She is a private person. I do not think she would appreciate me telling about her like this."

"And what about Abraham?" She turned to me, "You have been single for quite a long time. I do not think you have had any girlfriends in the last three years?" She asked me, "No, I have not had any girl." I shook my head.

"Why so?" She knitted her eyebrows, "Uh…I did not find the right girl I guess and yes, I love our fans way too much. I do not want to share the love I have with someone else." I laughed a bit.

Turning to the fans I saw a slightly sad expression on Scarlette's face; she looked up and gave a small smile. A smile that was sad and forced, "Though I know, one day I surely will find a girl who will take all the love from me and she will be the one who will really tell me that I am perfect." I smiled at her genuinely and she blushed.

Wait, what am I doing? Why am I doing this? She does not know anything about me and my past, why am I getting her hopes high? No, I have to stay away from her; I am not in love with her. She is only my friend.

"So is there any girl right now?" Sharlie asked me, I made up my mind and I knew what I was going to do would hurt her but to keep her happy in the future I will have to hurt her now.

I want to be the oxygen when she breathes, the reason of her smiles. However, I can just be the reason of her tears if I get too close to her…I have to stay away from her…And I will.

"Uh, duh. No not at all. The girls I know, except the fans, are not of that level you know!" I shrugged with a lot of attitude and from the corner of my eyes I could see defeat on her face while my heart broke in a million pieces.

"Ooooh! That only I thought how did you get all sweet and romantic?" She tossed sarcasm and all of them laughed including me. "Now let us hear the newest single of Groove!" She announced and the entire audience rose in applause.

We stood in a line and sung our new single "I wanna grow old with you".

"Like a feeling you can't explain.

Love can take your breath away.

Like the sun shining in the dawn,

Love brings your whole world down.

All I wanted now, I just wanna grow old with you.

Time will tell me how…

Suddenly everything has turned upside down

Suddenly love is the thing that I think most about…

You are my love, my happiness

I just wanna grow old with you…

You are the one that makes me laugh

When I'm low I know I have you…

Baby, I just wanna grow old with you…

God I love you now… I just wanna grown old with you

You can show me now

suddenly loves a thing…that I think….most about…"

I opened my eyes in the end as I did not want to look at Scarlette even though I was singing to her- I do not want to get her hopes high, I do not want to fall in love with her… I cannot fall in love with her.

Chapter 11

<u>Scarlette</u>

<u>*6 months later*</u>

It has been six months on the 'While we are' tour and I absolutely love being a part of the Groove crew. Moreover, Abraham and I have been really good friends, like, he is sweet to me and we hang out quite often so I guess we are friends.

I know I said I will not make any close friends but I feel something like a connection with him, as if we are meant to be around. However, he is not that close that I tell him about my condition. Not that I do not trust him, I whole heartedly trust him but I do not trust myself and my fate.

The same thing is with him. The Abraham Khan the world knows is not the real Abraham Khan not that I know him inside out, but sometimes if he is left alone or is playing guitar alone there a lost expression on his face, the one with dark eyes. He has a mask on his face, hiding something and getting hurt by something but not telling anyone.

Anyways, I am absolutely chilled out today as we have got a holiday and we are going to celebrate six months of the tour. We are going clubbing! After six tiring yet amazing months of touring we are finally going clubbing.

Suddenly my phone pinged breaking my chain of thoughts, '@ ShawnW19 tagged you in a picture.' My Instagram notification flashed on the notification panel. I clicked on it and opened it to reveal an adorable picture of the boys pouting and sitting in the car.

I laughed as I read the caption "@ScarletteJW you take so much time to get ready. Now we know why how you are always so beautiful! #WhenScarletteTakesTooLong #WaitingInTheCar #Been30mins #PoutyPeople!'

I face palmed and remembered that they were waiting down in the car for me. I quickly gave one last look as I stood in a nice little black dress, thick liner with a bright red lipstick, black bellies in the feet and hair in big curls.

I walked downstairs to the hotel lobby and from the glass door I could see camera flashes of the paparazzi. I called Abraham, "Scarlette where are you?" He asked quickly. "I am here Abraham but there is so much of paparazzi and no guards... how should I come?" I whined.

He sighed, "Wait, I am coming." He said and disconnected the call.

Within a few seconds I could see Abraham walk in the door, with his head down, he quickly entered. He looked kind of sexy in a white shirt, brown leather jacket and blue denim jeans.

"Hi." He looked up and greeted me with a smile, "Hi there." I smiled back as he eyed me. "You look good!" He said in an appreciative tone and I nodded with a grin in reply.

"Ready? Just keep your head down and walk without tripping yeah?" He asked unsurely and I nodded. He wrapped his arms around my waist and we hastily walked to the car.

As we sat down, I was almost blinded by all the flashes. "Damn, that was too bright." I said as I widened my eyes and all of them laughed.

"Uh uhm Scarlette, you look very uhm pretty today." Jacob spoke hesitantly from the driver's seat; I could see Shawn smiling goofily next to him and Abraham frowning next to me.

"Thank you Jacob." I said in a low voice with a small smile. I do not really like him, I mean he is sweet and everything but what he did seven months back and even though I said that I have forgiven him there is something in me really has not.

Jacob drove the car, Shawn on the passenger's seat, Mark and Oliver at the back and Abraham and I on the middle seats. It was a nice and big SUV that I was saving money for.

All through the ride the boys danced and sung almost all the songs on the CD player, cracking me up on their hilarious dance moves and Shawn's made up cranky voice. As we reached the NA Party House all we saw at first was paparazzi and all we heard first was our sighs behind the camera flashes.

"Look at the privacy killers!" Mark said in a dramatic tone while all of us laughed. "Let us do this!" Oliver said and all of us got down the car with our heads down and quickly walked to the door.

"Tada! We did it!" I spoke in a shrill voice as if we won some big game and all of us clapped and laughed at the same time. "Want to have a dance?" Jacob asked me with his hand out, I gulped hard, "Uh Jacob uhm, sorry but dance is really not my thing. My legs and hands move in totally different directions. I am sorry but no." He gave him an apologetic smile even though I am a dancer.

It hurt me to say no to him because he became sad. I did not reject the proposal because I do not like him, I rejected it because I know it can be fatal for me and I am not in a state to tell about my condition to anyone.

Suddenly we were interrupted by a number of fan girls and I quickly excused myself to the bar, I really do not want to be crushed to death under excited teenage girls.

"Hi Scarlette, What's up in life?" Suddenly Jacob spoke as he sat next to me, "Nothing special. You say?" I looked down at the neon blue illuminated bar table. "I am in love." He replied slowly and I chuckled, "Really? Who?" I grinned at him and looked down again.

"I in love with you Scarlette." He replied as my eyes went wide at him, I spun and faced him, "Sorry, what?" I asked in confusion.

My eyes were wide and on the verge of popping out, my palms were sweating and adrenaline was kicking in me. He cannot be serious. Is he? He is? Huh? No.

He took a deep breath, "Yes, I am in love with you Scarlette. Yes, I know what I did was stupidity and a very evil thing to do to a living being but I really did not know that you were such an amazing girl. Yes, I felt a connection with you but you always avoided me. Yes, a big and deep pit of jealousy explodes in me whenever I see you and Abraham together. Yes, you take my breath away each time you enter the green room or when you just walk in and talk to us. Yes, I cannot control these feelings and emotions anymore Scar, I want to claim you as mine. Will you be my girlfriend?" He said looking into my eyes that were out of their sockets.

He had a soft and expectant expression on his face; his eyes were brighter than the stars and face illuminated with a sweet expression. I *will* have to break his heart, for his happy future I will do this.

"Uh, Jacob. Actually uhm I never really felt anything towards you other than friendship. I see you as my friend and I am not really ready for a relationship, I want to work hard first, I have my family to keep up with. I am sorry Jacob but I cannot be your girlfriend." I sighed looking down.

"No freaking girl says *no* to Jacob San Tiago," Suddenly Jacob spoke through gritted teeth. I looked up to witness a completely different Jacob than what I saw seconds before. He had a tough and angry expression on his face, "You bitch," He spit and I just stared at him with a confused face.

"Jacob?" I held his arm but he jerked it away, "You think you are the only one? You think Jacob San Tiago has got only you? No, you little bitch! I have got millions of girls after me who are way better than you. You slut! You bonded with Shawn at the office then you went on a date with me and even kissed me but after that you wooed Abraham and made him yours. You spent a night in his room. God knows what you two did! You took Abraham, my one time best friend, away from me! He hates me because of you! I hate you Scarlette John Waters, you are useless! No one like you! Abraham is not interested in you, he just cares for everyone. You are bullshit!" He yelled on my face.

Tears were there in my eyes by the time Jacob finished his rant and walked away. I turned around to see people whispering to each other. In frustration, shame and anger I could understand nothing; I chucked down three mugs of beer and still cried due to his words.

Wait, where is Abraham? I turned to look around and saw him standing with a beautiful girl and talking to her. She was holding his arm and then his shoulder. He was not into me. No one likes me, I am useless. Slowly and slowly, Jacob's words were swimming around and tattooing themselves on the walls of my mind and heart, they made the water flow from my eyes.

Due to the dizziness and tipsiness from the beer I felt as though I was no more on Earth. The place was absolutely insane. There were people wherever my eyes could look, drinking, smoking, yelling, dancing, kissing. The music was suddenly too loud and the lights were too dim and strobe like.

I went to the dance floor after a nice stumbling and falling, the alcohol had taken the best out of me. Everything around me started to blur into one collective image, and I felt a little funny. I started moving around to the beat and danced wildly. I did not recognize the song at all. I didn't even think it is a song, just some electric music. But it seemed that everyone liked it very much.

I lost myself completely in the music, and felt free. I felt as though I am not myself and somehow I liked that. I was a dancer but due to my condition I could never dance in public. But nothing stopped me at that time of point of time, I was too angry and depressed with myself.

As I did my wild moves, suddenly I felt my breath giving up my lungs and dizziness covered my brain and eyes. I knew this would happen and I was absolutely ready for it. I started to feel light and all my body started panting. I was grasping for breath and I was coughing blood on my handkerchief. Slowly I lost control over my body and was about to fall on the ground.

Suddenly, I stumble and fell onto someone, who catches me quickly and holds me steadily in his arms. His arms were warm and familiar. They were big, soft and nice arms, the ones that had provided me home before. I look up and look right at the person, Abraham.

Abraham had a worried expression written all over his face, "Scarlette?" He spoke as my vision started to blur, "Ambulance-" And then everything went black.

Chapter 12

<u>Abraham</u>

"Come back home, Abraham," My little cousin Alisha held my arm.

"We miss you." She requested. "I cannot come back after what happened. I will not be able to see Zara aunt's face after what happened due to me." I looked down in shame.

"Nothing happened due to you Abraham. Destiny is to be blamed, not you. It was supposed to happen." She held my shoulder in comfort.

"No Alisha. All happened due to me, I wish I could rewind everything. I would have everything- my family, my friends, everything…Sarah." I looked up at her. "You do not have to bla-"

Both of us suddenly spotted someone on the dance floor. She was a beautiful girl dressed in a little black dress and looked absolutely stunning as she danced her heart out and I must say, she was a total professional dancer. She was really good and I envied her a bit.

"Abraham, that girl is so awesome. Let us go see who she is!" Alisha insisted, changing the topic and I nodded as she accompanied me towards the dance floor. On a closer view I realized the girl had a striking resemblance with someone, someone I knew really well but could not click.

All of a sudden she paused, her back facing me, she was looking as if she was struggling to catch her breath as was coughing badly and I could see blood coming on her handkerchief.

I walked to help her and as I held her cold arms I realized who she was…Scarlette.

"Scarlette?" I spoke to her as her eyes started closing, "Ambulance-" she uttered in between coughs and soon fainted in my arms. Unable to understand anything else I carried her bridal style, in my arms and took her to the car.

"Abraham, what even happened?" Mark stopped me midway, "Sh-she fainted. I do not know. Give me the car keys!" I said hurriedly. He searched for the keys into his pocket and handed them to me without another word and I quickly ran to the car.

Reaching the car I carefully put her in the passenger's seat, put the seat belt and kissed her forehead. I ran to the driver's seat and drove to the 'Peter and co Hollywood Hospital', our hospital, the one reserved for celebrities.

I know I could get a speeding ticket for driving above 70 but nothing else matter to me more than Scarlette and her life at that point. All through the 5 minutes ride I held her freezing hand and kept kissing it. *She* matters to me the most.

Soon a feeling of déjà vu hit me, the fainting, the fast driving, the worries…the hospital.

I parked the car and picked her up again, in my fastest possible pace, I ran to the door of the hospital. "Emergency ward, quick!" I said to the receptionist, "Sorry sir we cannot admit her. She's not a celebrity or related to one, she is a stylist." The receptionist spoke emotionlessly and I so badly wanted to yell on her but I didn't.

"I am Abraham Khan from Groove and she is Scarlette Waters my…m-my…*girlfriend.*" I forced my words, somehow I felt uncomfortable calling her my girlfriend, it was not right but I had to do it to save her.

"Oh I am sorry Mr. Khan. We will do the arrangements." They quickly brought a stretcher in front of me and I landed Scarlette carefully on it. They hurriedly took her to ICU at the fifth floor, "What happened to her sir?" The doctor asked to me.

"I-I do not know doc, she was dancing then she suddenly started struggling for breath and fainted. Please save her, please."

Before I could realize tears were stinging my eyes, "She is in the ICU but… We will try our best sir." He said and quickly walked away to the Intensive Care Unit on the fifth floor.

I went to the lift and pressed the '5' button. I looked at a couple standing next to me who was holding a little baby of about a few days in their arms, "Is she a baby girl?" I couldn't help but ask them. "Yes." The father smiled at me, "What is her name?" I asked her, "Maria Sholes. I am a fan of your band, you had a song called Maria and so I named her Maria." The mother spoke and kissed the baby girl. It surprises me how much just a single song of ours can save so many lives yet so many lives cannot save one.

"How did you get permission to deliver her here? I do not think I have seen both of you in some celebrity type thing." I asked hesitantly and the lady smiled at me, "My name is Nicola Stephens and I am Peter Devine's step daughter." She held her hand out at me and I shook it in surprise. I smiled at them and walked out as the lift reached the fifth floor.

I sat outside the door when my phone rang. "Hello." I spoke without seeing the Caller ID, "Where on Earth are you Abraham Khan?" Alisha's scream traveled through the phone. "I am at the Peter hospital Alisha." I muttered as I realized I did not inform her while leaving with Scarlette.

"Hospital?" Her voice quickly calmed down, "Why? What happened?" She spoke with her voice laced with concern. "You remember that girl who was dancing there?" I asked and she hummed in response, "She is my friend and she is in the hospital" I felt my heart drop, "I just…I do not know what to do Alisha. If anything…If anything happens to her…" Without another thought tears started flowing out of my eyes and I did not stop them.

"Oh God! I am sorry for yelling at you like this please stay calm. I got so worried seeing you not around. I see you are quite concerned. She'll be okay Abraham I know...But you know what you are doing, right?" She spoke the last part in a low tone with a little emphasis on 'you', "I don't know anything Alisha. I only want Scarlette's safety right now." I confessed.

"I trust you Abraham. Bye and Scarlette will soon be alright Inshallah." She spoke to me in concern before leaving me with a monotonous beep and sweating palms.

I sat confined by the hospital walls on the chair, just waiting and waiting for the door to my left to open and the doctor to emerge. My stomach was twisting at all the possibilities running through my mind. The lights in the hospital were blinding, and they reflected pain off the plain white walls and it was hurting to look at them. But I kept looking. My eyes were sore and dry but I was still scared and in pain.

As soon as I turned to the door, the doctor came out from the ICU, "How is she?" I asked him hurriedly, "How can you be so irresponsible Mr. Khan?" The doctor scolded me with a frown on his face. "Excuse me?" I spoke as clouds of confusion covered my brain.

"How can you let your girlfriend dance when she is in this condition?" He spoke in wonder making me more confused than ever, he said girlfriend because I said that at the reception. "She did not tell me anything, we have been together only for a week. Why what is wrong?" I asked him clearly.

"She went out of breath Mr. Khan! As told by her, she was born immature and her mother had a lot of complications during her pregnancy. Ms. Scarlette has one of her lungs only developed half; it shut down due to such wild dancing. A lot of crying, dancing or heavy work can lead to her death. She cannot handle heavy breathing; you need to be with her at this time Mr. Khan." He stated with worry and I almost understood what he meant.

My breathing slowed down as I realized there was such a thing Scarlette did not tell me, and I did not know what pained more, that fact that she did not tell me or that fact that she did not trust me enough. This was what was killing her bit by bit, this was what she thought I would not understand, and that was her secret.

However, now that I know, I have understood that I cannot face all that again. I cannot lose the person I love again. I cannot let her go again. Once was more than enough, it took me three years to revive, not again.

"Will she live?" I asked him in a choking voice, "Yes she may, not sure but she may. She has chances if she gets operated in two years she will live." He reassured me as a wave of happiness went through me, "You can go and meet her if you want." He smiled at me because I guess he knew I would ask him to.

"Uh can I take her to the balcony? I know she is stressed and she will want to go to the balcony." I bit my lip nervously, he nodded in response, "Yes you can. But she is very weak right now, you need to keep holding her and give her your jacket." He smiled at me.

The old doctor then started to walk away, suddenly he stopped and faced me, "Take care of her and do not make her cry." He beamed at me and turned back again.

Scarlette is the greatest and loveliest of all creatures, flawless in spite of all her flaws and I love her for who she is.

Chapter 13

<u>Scarlette</u>

I regret dancing at the club, now I know that Abraham knows my secret, something that was not supposed to tell people. I don't want pity and donation from people. I want to be normal and I don't want to hurt anyone after I die. That is why I never told Abraham or anyone about my illness except my family and Augustus. I don't deserve love.

Suddenly there was a knock on the door breaking my chain of thoughts, "Come in." I said slowly and the door opened revealing Abraham. He entered in the room looking down and I knew none of us was ready to face the other. Maybe he was surprised and shocked but I felt as though I had betrayed him.

We just kept quiet, looking at the floor, the air thick and heavy and full of pain and questions. From the corner of my eyes, I could see him running a hand through his hair and looking at the floor; as if trying to pull him together.

In that moment, I notice every single of his body movements. I notice the shaking of his fingers, the quick rise and fall of his chest and the biting of his lip. I notice the anxiety and fear. The complete and utter fear.

Slowly he looked up at me and the mere sight of his face broke my heart into a million pieces. His eyes were red, glassy and swollen. It was evident that he had been crying, his hands were shaking and his hair was ruffled. He kept looking at me with a blank and numb expression as a small tear, escaped its way out from his eyes.

After what seemed like forever he spoke, "Wan-" he croaked and cleared his throat, "Want to go to the b-balcony?" He sobbed. I nodded slowly and tried to get up. "I got you." He walked to me and helped me up. I slowly got up and with his help, walked to a door that opened to the balcony. He helped me sit, on a bench placed, near the railing and stood next to me. For a solid five minutes, we kept looking at everything but each other.

"London is beautiful," he spoke suddenly making me look at him. I nodded silently in reply. "Everything, everyone and every incident isn't beautiful. However, we live with it-" He looked at me, "We share it with the people who give a damn." I knew what he meant and I quickly looked down.

"Why didn't you tell me, Scarlette?" I felt weight rise on the bench next to me.

"W-what are you talking about?" I mumbled.

"You know exactly what I am talking about."

He stated simply, "Now you know about it right? That's it."

There were no guts in me that would make me look at him in the eye.

"Look at me Scar..." He said holding my hand, his touch sent electric shocks in my body and before I knew I was sitting face to face with him. "What happened to you?" He asked, "I know the doctor has already told you about me. Why are you asking me?" I spoke in a low voice.

"Because you do not give a shit about what I would feel," He said in an irritated tone and took a deep breath, "I want to hear it from you. I do not know anything. Tell me." He sighed and I nodded.

"Let us have a clause: We will disclose our secrets. Tell each other 'something' from our lives. Like, you want to know this and I also want to know something. Ok?" I stated.

His jaw tightened, he thought for a bit before nodding. "But you will tell first." He raised his index finger at me.

I agreed.

"I was born pre-mature. Due to the complications during the delivery, my one lung is only half developed which makes it difficult to breath when I do heavy work or I dance or cry. This disease is called respiratory distress syndrome. I have to go for getting the water removed from my lungs every eight months. This can be cured by an operation if done within two years but I cannot afford that. I don't want to become a charity case so I did not tell anybody about my health. But I am happy Abraham. I am okay with this disease. I don't have a reason to live. I don't want any sympathy or pity. I want to be normal. I want the least number of people to cry on my funeral. That day is not far when I'll di-" I was interrupted with his warm and bone crushing, bear hug. The one that made this world feel like a better place to live in.

"Please don't go Scarlette," He cried as he nuzzled his face in my neck, "Hey Abraham shh, stop crying, I am not going anywhere. I am here with you." He looked up at me with this unbelievable kind of faith in his eyes.

"I cannot let you go Scarlette, I-I cannot break down again. You will not leave me, Promise?" I knew I was lying but to keep his heart from breaking I had to say yes, "Yes Abraham, I promise. I will always be with you, till *infinity*."

As a million stars light up the night, so was his face. He wiped away his tears. "Sorry, now it's your turn to ask me anything."

He chuckled at his emotional breakdown but I really did not find it funny.

If crying made his heart light, it was okay to cry.

This is the reason I love rains, they tell us that it is okay to cry and let out things kept inside you from a long time, because even the sky does. Mother Nature has her own way of venting out. Earthquakes, storms, rains and volcanic eruptions are ways she vents out her pain. If it is natural for nature to vent out so is it for the humans. But we choose to keep it inside and instead live with a mask of bravery and strength, even while we die from within bit by bit, every single day.

It was my turn to ask him about someone and something. I have been dying to ask since last three months. I remember the incident that happened three months ago:

"Truth or dare Scarlette?" Mark wiggled his eyebrows as I thought for a bit. I was playing truth and dare with the boys for the first time. "Dare!" I beamed and he nodded at me before naughtily looking at Shawn.

"You and Abraham have to sleep together for a night." He spoke making me and Abraham to look at each other with eyes so wide that they would have popped out. "Uh how about no?" Abraham spoke as he choked on his spit after reviving from the shock, "Uhm yeah I do not think we will do it." I muttered.

"You just have to sleep together. Only sleep nothing else. *wink*." Shawn said boldly. I found myself growing red, in embarrassment. "Uhm okay, let us do this." Abraham shrugged and got up, taking me by shock as he gave his hand to me, "Come, let us go." He smirked and I too got up.

"That is the spirit baby!" Oliver yelled and I rolled my eyes at him.

We went and lay down next to one another and before I realized Abraham had already fallen asleep. As I was about to close my eyes when Abraham muttered, "Sarah."

"Don't leave me Sarah." Tears started flowing from his eyes as he started moving his hands in the air.

~ ~ ~

I know what I have to ask him today.

Chapter 14

<u>Abraham</u>

Scarlette is one of the strongest people, I have ever known. Despite knowing that she would die, sooner than many others she kept herself positive and is still chirpy. Here, I am- looking for an anchor in her. There she is facing the world without a fear of death.

"Sorry, now it is your turn to ask me anything." I wiped away my tears and smiled sheepishly. She was too drifted off in her own world. Her eyes were set on the floor and she was drifted in her own deep thoughts.

"Scarlette?" I touched her shoulder and she jumped in her place. "Sorry, I was thinking something." She gave a small smile.

"Now ask if you want to." I flashed a smile at her and she nodded.

"Look, I have been thinking to ask about this since the last three months but I never expected a reply from you. I know, it is a very personal thing but I want to know because you always take my name when I talk about that thing." She said with closed eyes.

"You ask whatever you want to." I reassured her without a second thought and she nodded.

Spending seven months with her, I have understood a few things about her. She talks a lot but most of her conversations comprises of nods, sighs and deep breaths.

Another peculiar thing about her is her movement of eyes. She loves to roll her eyes, close them and raise her eyebrows.

"Who is Sarah?" She spoke and suddenly my head felt dizzy. How does she know about Sarah? No one is supposed to know her, us and the history we share. It is dark and I don't want any light in there. I just want to rewind the events. Sometimes, it is better to live in the dark than to be blinded by the lights.

"I-I do not know any Sarah." I faced the ground, her hands came in contact with my shoulder, "Firstly, you know you cannot lie and secondly, this is the reason I wasn't telling you about my illness. I knew you wouldn't answer me. Just… Forget it Abraham, forget all this ever happened and I ever told you anything." She turned to walk away.

"Sarah was my love." I spoke suddenly and she turned to me with a concerned look on her face. "She was my ex-girlfriend;

chuck it, my only girlfriend. You know in my religion you can marry your cousin. She was my cousin." I looked up at her.

"Where is she and why did you two break up then?" She asked in disbelieve.

"Sh-she is no-more." I muttered and soon felt tears stinging my eyes.

"She is no …more? Oh my God, I am so sorry." She spoke with regret and sadness in her voice, walked to me and hugged me, as I cried a little.

"It is okay. I don't want to know anything. Forget it but please stop crying. Please." She rubbed my back; sat down with me on the and within those few seconds I made the first proper decision of my life.

I will tell Scarlette everything about Sarah.

"No, I will tell you. It's pretty long." I said as I pulled back, "Stop wherever you feel uncomfortable, I don't have a problem." She gave me a small and sympathetic smile.

I took a deep breath with closed eyes as my life flashed like a movie in front of my eyes, the life changing events that occurred three years back.

"Sarah Zaidi, my maternal aunt's daughter, my childhood friend and my only girlfriend. We were deeply in love, even though my mother did not support our relationship. I loved her with everything I had without knowing that I would lose everything I had soon..." I gulped.

"One day my entire family was celebrating Eid and all of my cousins were there. Reyaan Saeed, my brother was there too and I was closest to him. We were just chilling. Reyaan's parents died in a car accident some years back and hence he lived with us. He was the best brother one could ever ask for.

It was great fun being in a joint family, big happy family with many cousins to play with. All of a sudden one of my little cousins Zehra Khan, my paternal uncle's daughter, she came running to me and my older sister Adina, "Abraham and Adina come in quickly, Sarah has fainted. Aunt is calling you both."

Both I and my sister were terrified, so we ran inside to our mother, Mrs. Noor Azhaar Khan, "Take her to the hospital, quick!" She yelled and then we realized that being the oldest kids in the clan. We were expected to take carry Sarah in the car and to the hospital.

I drove as fast as I could and took Sarah to the City hospital, Bradford. There we put her into the emergency ward where the doctor did her checkup. After a couple of minutes or rather years he came out of the room and looked at me, "Are you Ms. Zaidi's husband?" Being young, I first blushed but finally spoke, "No sir, her boyfriend." He gave me the biggest grin and spoke, "Congratulations sir, Ms. Zaidi's pregnant." He spoke and my jaw fell on the floor.

In my religion, it is an evil deed to have a child before marriage and I was more shocked than anything in the world. We had never been into such physical relationship ever. We hail from an orthodox background. We had a pact to indulge in such a thing have sex, only after marriage. Here I was, hearing from the doctor, that my girlfriend was pregnant.

"She's what?" Her mother and my aunt, Zara Zaidi, yelled in shock. While all others stared at me in disbelief

"Ms. Zaidi is pregnant." The doctor repeated with confusion written all over his face.

"B-but aunt we hav-" I tried to speak.

"Shut up Abraham! Just shut up!" Zara aunt raised her hand to silence me.

"Please stay silent ma'am." The nurse held her hand.

"Silent? Do hell with you!" She yelled and walked away in a huff.

Every single thing in my body was heavy. It was sinking to the floor and replacing me with emptiness. I could not understand what she was saying, and I understood only one thing that it was not true. She cannot. She cannot be saying what I was hearing her say. Sarah betrayed me. Did she?

"You have embarrassed the family so much Abraham!" Mum held my shoulder. I was too engulfed by the shock and a small feeling of betrayal to look at my mother. All I wanted to do or to see was no one else but Sarah Zaidi. I wanted explanations. I wanted *answers*.

"I-I know we have not done anything." I sighed as I finally found the guts to speak up, "Then how did she get pregnant? By sperm donation?" Mum spoke and soon her hands came in contact with my cheek and left a stinging pain.

"You ask her. She will tell you we have not done anything!" I spoke as tears started flowing down my cheeks and mum walked away.

"Can we meet her?" I heard Reyaan's voice for the very first time since Sarah fainted as he spoke to the nurse, "Yes but only three people at once." She spoke and walked away.

"I want to meet her." I raised my hand and started to walk to the door. A hand held my collar, "I will not let my daughter be alone with you anymore Abraham Khan." Zara aunt spoke through gritted teeth and was about to hit me when Reyaan stepped in.

"Aunt, please stop; let us talk to Sarah about it first." He held aunt's hand and opened the door to let us walk in.

"Sarah!" Aunt yelled as soon as she entered, "Aunt please, she is not very strong. Relax!" Reyaan held aunt's shoulder and calmed her down.

Reyaan's sudden caring and sweet attitude came as a surprise to me. He was not the kind of guy who would care for someone. I sensed fear in his eyes but did not push further, because the situation was at its worst.

"Abraham." Sarah spoke in a small voice and the look on her face was apologetic. Her face was pale, her eyes were stinging pink from all the tears and her perfect lips were in a shade of blue. All I could see in her eyes was pain and guilt. In that little eye contact, I understood that she was hiding something from me. She was lying.

"What did you do Sarah!? Didn't you think about Allah or our reputation before doing such a dirty thing with Abraham? Why did you do this?" Aunt shot questions at her without any pause. She just looked at her white hands. "Who is the father of this child Sarah Zaidi?" She howled without giving her a chance to answer.

Sarah looked up with pain in her eyes, "Mum uhm the child's father is-" the pain in her eyes was suddenly covered by utter fear, and she turned immensely scared and gulped hard.

"Abraham." She said and my jaw literally dropped on the floor with my eyeballs out of my eye sockets. I was not surprised or shocked but I was hurt. She was lying in front of me. She is cheating on me, in my face.

"Sarah why are you lying?" I asked her in disbelief.

"Why are *you* lying Abraham? Remember last month we did it? You didn't use any protection!" She shot back at me and I almost fell down. Sarah was the girl who could never lie. The girl who would not sleep in the night, if she lied to her teacher about not having a pen when she had it. She was too rigid on having a pure 'deen'. This was the most selfless and honest person ever and she were lying on my face.

After that, till about a week I was not allowed to talk to Sarah or any of my cousins. I was blamed for doing something I was never really responsible of doing.

One night, after drinking, having taken enough of all the treatment I went over to Sarah's room but as I almost reached there. I saw Reyaan coming out of her room with anger dripping from his eyes. "Reyaan! Reyaan! I cannot do that!

Reyaan!" Sarah yelled from inside with a voice that was soaked in tears but he did not stop.

I instantly understood there was something wrong.

I quietly opened the door and entered the room, "Sarah!?" I yelled at what I saw. I ran to her, she was sitting on the couch crying her eyes out.

Her white suit all crushed and crumpled. Her eyes red, cheeks drenched with tears and pain. Her makeup was entirely smudged; her kohl was dripping, ruining her suit. She appeared so vulnerable and broken. I had never seen her that way before.

"Baby what's wrong? Please tell me." I kneeled down to her level, all my angry and frustration had flown out of the window.

"Abraham I-I have to tell you something. I am sorry Abraham but you are not the reason for the things I have been blaming you for." Sarah hiccupped. Her beautiful face was all red and swollen. I looked into her bloodshot eyes which were filled with guilt.

"Who did this Sarah?" I asked her on the verge of tears. She sobbed and wiped her eyes.

"The person who ruined me is no one else but Reyaan. This child is my and Reyaan's." She spoke and broke down in another fit of tears.

"H-How is this possible? You are in love with Reyaan?" I asked her in a low voice.

She casted her eyes down and confessed, "No Abraham. I love you and only you."

"Then how did you get pregnant with him?" I asked with nothing but clouds of confusion covering my head making it unable to process anything.

"Reyaan raped me." She spoke and in an instant my brain and body froze.

"He what?" I exclaimed after trying to absorb the situation but failing miserably.

Reyaan was my best friend cum brother and he doing such a thing with my girlfriend. This was something that came like a massive shock to me. Never in my worst imaginations had I imagined that my own brother would do such a thing to me.

"Yes, last month when I was hanging out with him he took me for a drink which I gladly accepted unaware to the fact that the drink which I was assuming to be lemonade had sleeping pills mixed in them.

Next day when I woke up I was in a room, lying naked on the bed with him. He was also naked.

When I woke up and asked him what happened! He told me that he did all that to take my virginity away from me before you could do that. If only I knew he was not an angel but a devil...If only I knew that he would be the one to do something like that to me." She broke down again and buried her face in her hands.

"Why didn't you tell everyone in the hospital that day Sarah?" I asked her, kneeling down in front of her.

She looked up at me, "Reyaan forced me to shut up. He had c-clicked pictures of me. That day as I looked up at you, he glared at me and flashed a nude picture of me on his phone. I was helpless Abraham." She hugged me and started crying again.

The next thing I did was something I regret the most. I wish I had not done that. Things would have been way different than what they are today if I had just quietly walked out of her room.

In anger and under the influence of alcohol I pushed her away from me, "You are such a selfish person Sarah Zaidi! You took my name just because Reyaan did it and you got pregnant. Are you hearing yourself? How selfish can you be Sarah? Did you think this for even a second that how would it affect my life? My future? My relations with the other family members? Just because of you and your lie. Zara aunt doesn't want to see my face, for no reason she hates me. I would have always backed you Sarah if you could have used your rotten brain and told me about the rape beforehand instead of blaming me for this goddamn deed! You are so selfish Sarah, go to hell!" I yelled on her face and left her room, banging the door.

As soon as I exited I came face to face with the person I least wanted to say at that time, Reyaan Saeed.

"How could you do that to me Reyaan? You are my own brother dude, I considered you as my best friend and this is what you do to a brother? You rape their girlfriend?" I asked him in disbelief as I expected a sorry in reply.

However, you do not get what you expect. The world is not a romantic movie in which everything goes as expected with a happy ending. Instead of begging for forgiveness, he smirked at me, "This is what happens when you think you are way too great."

He spoke and I stared at him with confusion, "Ever since we were kids you got all the attention, you can sing, you can draw well and you look better than me doesn't mean I won't be given any attention. All the girls used to go bananas over you at school, our parents always liked to hear you sing, you are being trained to go to the Voice of UK audition this year. I had a crush on Sarah but she fell for you and you both started dating. What about me Abraham? What have I ever got? Nothing! Absolutely nothing! I decided to hurt you on the part where it would hurt you the most. Your only weakness is Sarah Zaidi. Now you cannot do anything and are stuck with this problem!" He smiled wickedly at me. I thought where my best friend had gone?

Little had I known, he had just arrived.

I could not believe my ears, my best friend. My brother had done such a low thing just because he was jealous of me. He ruined my and my girlfriend's life, just for the sake of his jealousy. I trusted this boy since the last 21 years.

Not wanting to beat the shit out of him and wake the others up. I pushed him away before going up the stairs and walking away to my room, fuming with anger.

I looked around at my and Reyaan's pictures hanging on the walls and punched each one of them. I had trusted him so much and I so badly wanted to rewind things and tell my old self to stop trusting him because at the end he will be the one ruining our life.

Before going to sleep I called my cousin Alisha Khan, my paternal uncle's daughter, seeing the clock strike at 2am I disconnected it. She is the only sister after Sarah and my little sibling Yasmin, with whom, I can discuss anything. Without the fear of the thing being a center of gossips. Here, Sarah was the only one I had to talk about and I did not find it appropriate to discuss such things with my 16 year old little sister. I called Alisha. As I was about to fall asleep my phone rang. *Alisha* the Caller ID flashed. "You called?" she asked before yawning as soon as I pressed the phone to my ear.

"Uh n-nothing, by mistake." I managed to speak in such a way that it appeared that I was normal.

"Are you crying? Abraham what's up? What's bothering you?" She spoke quickly as if she read my mind and knew that I was shattered. "I am so fucked up Alisha!" Before I could realize I was bursting in tears and crying.

"Abraham please keep calm, I am coming downstairs."

She spoke hurriedly before disconnecting the call and within seconds there was a knock on my room's door, "Yeah." I managed to speak.

The door opened revealing an Alisha in a pink nighty and brown hair in a ponytail, "Why on Earth are you caterwauling Abraham?" She ran to me before engulfing me in a hug with a worried expression her face. I told her the entire incident and how confused I was on what I should do.

She sighed and sat on beanbag, next to me.

"You know why she took your name instead of just taking some random name?" She asked me and I shook my head.

"I'll tell you. She did so because she trusts you Abraham. She knows that if anyone who can help and accept her in such a situation exists, it's you Abraham Khan." She smiled at me and brought her knees in front of her chest and wrapped her arms around them as she stared at the floor.

"Life is all about giving everything to that one person who completes your life, she finds that person in you. Sarah wanted a name for her child therefore, she took your name."

She turned to me, "Don't let her down Abraham. Accept her and this child. Maybe he or she will complete you both. Marry Sarah." She hugged me.

"Promise me you will not tell anyone about Reyaan and Sarah." I ordered and she nodded.

"I promise. This thing is between you and me." She smiled at me.

I do not know how but for the very first time I was making the best decision of my life.

"I will propose her tomorrow." I grinned, "Empty handed?"

She rose her eyebrows, seeing a sad expression on my face she chuckled, "Give her this ring; I bought it for her so that she feels good. However, I suppose you giving it to her makes more sense." She grinned and handed me a beautiful ring from her pocket.

"You know you are the best sister, right Alisha?" I grinned while admiring the ring, "Lol yes, I *am* the best sister. You are so lucky Khan!" She said and before knowing a chuckle escaped my lips.

"Now you go to sleep. It is five in the morning and I don't want you to propose your girlfriend with eye bags okay?" she hugged me again before getting up.

"Good night Abraham, sleep tight, take care and all the best." She grinned and walked away as quietly as she had come." I opened my eyes slowly.

Chapter 15

<u>Abraham</u>

"So did she say yes?" Scarlette asked me, breaking my chain of thoughts as a little tear escaped my eyes.

"She did not say anything. She just went away." More tears found their way out.

"Look, if you don't wa-" I stopped her, "I will." I wiped my tears away, took a deep breath and started again.

"Next morning I got up at around eight and got dressed in a nice white shirt and blue jeans. I was very happy and was going to make that day the best day of our lives, not knowing that the same day would be the worst day of my life.

I went down the stairs to see everyone working around, I looked at Alisha, who had big dark circles, and asked her about Sarah's whereabouts. "In her room." She mouthed and I nodded. She traced the shape of a ring on her ring finger and raised her eyebrows. I glanced towards Sarah's room door and she grinned in reply, hiding from our mothers in the kitchen she gave me a thumbs up and I bowed slightly in reply.

I took a deep breath and entered Sarah's room quietly, "Sarah!" I spoke in a low volume. No reply.

"Sarah?" I called again.

"Sarah!" I called again this time slightly louder.

Me- *Where is Sarah?*

Alisha- *In her room!*

Me- *Oh my God! Wow, thanks Sherlock -_-*

Alisha- *Fuck you Abraham! I don't know, she never came out of her room. Might be in the washroom, don't just barge in huh? ;)*

Me- *Eww Alisha! Anyways I'm going to propose her. Wish me luck bitch!*

Alisha- *Whatever -_-*

Not classifying her 'whatever -_-' important enough to reply. I shoved my phone back into my pocket and knocked on the washroom door.

No reply.

I knocked harder only to get the door already open, I opened the door fully and collapsed on the floor after what met my sight."

"Hey Abraham relax!" Scarlette hugged me as tears started flowing down my cheeks.

"I cannot forget her Scarlette. I cannot forget that sight." I mumbled in her hair.

"It's okay, don't remember it." She comfortingly rubbed my back.

I straightened up, "I have promised myself to tell you everything." Seeing I was in no mood to give up. She nodded helplessly in reply.

"As I opened the door I looked down and saw a red pool near my shoes. I looked up to see Sarah and in that fraction of seconds I could see my life, come shattering down. She was lying down near the bath tub, in one hand she held a blade and the other one's wrist had several deep cuts that had blood oozing out of them.

Her face was so calm and peaceful, as if she had given up all her worries and sadness and somehow a part of me understood that living was more painful to her than death. I had given her pain in life. I did not feel sad or depressed. I felt empty and numb. No feeling came in me; I was numb and was not ready to face that. I had killed Sarah. She committed suicide because of me. Before I could realize a loud scream escaped my mouth and I was in a pool of tears. I was a heap of mess. The tears flowing out of my eyes were mixing with the pool of Sarah's blood.

Suddenly my entire family was in front of my eyes, picking Sarah up and rushing to the hospital. I had no guts to face them or look at a dead Sarah. I did not go to the hospital to see her body or meet my family. I kept staining my pillow cover with the tears that never stopped until the black day came; it was the day Sarah had to be buried.

"Abraham?" Yasmin knocked at the door of my room.

"Hmm." I managed to reply in between tears.

"Come outside, mum is calling you, Sarah has to be buried…"

She spoke and that voice of hers was different, she was not in her usual chirpy and shrill voiced. Her voice was thick and somewhat tear soaked.

"Yasmi?" I called her by her nickname and looked up. The sight of her face wanted me to jump off and die. Her always bright eyes were scarily dark and red. Her nose that was always scrunched up in naughtiness was red and swollen. She was not smiling but was looking at me with…hate. I knew she loved Sarah a lot but the hatred filled expression was a bit weird to me.

"Yasmin Yaser Khan not Yasmi." She spoke with voice laced in disgust, "Yasmin what's up with you?" I asked her in confusion.

"Nothing, mum is calling you, just come." She had never spoken to me in that voice, even when I had forgotten her birthday last year.

"You hate me?" I asked her in a low voice, she took a deep breath, "Mum is calling you." She repeated, "I will not come until you answer me." I shook my head.

"Yes, I hate you Abraham." She spitted, "What do you expect huh? Just because of your lust; you have broken the entire family into fragments, you killed Sarah. Sarah! The light of the family. You blew the light away and left us into darkness. I loved you Abraham. I was so proud to move around and say Abraham Khan is my sibling but now I am really ashamed to even take your name. You come and see the situation of the house outside, mum and Zara aunt don't want to see each other's faces. Dad and Sarah's father Rehman uncle have not even exchanged a word. The worst situation is Alisha's mother Roohi aunt's, she has no idea whom she should console mum or Zara aunt. Reyaan, Adina, Zehra, Alisha or any of the kids have not spoken a word since yesterday. We have never stopped crying. All because of you Abraham!" She yelled at me as she broke into tears.

"Now stop doing this drama and come out, mum is calling you." She repeated as she wiped her eyes with the back of her hand and walked away. Yasmin is never able to make me feel guilty but that day she was successful. I felt guilty of breaking apart the family and killing Sarah.

I washed my face and quietly went down the stairs. The situation of the house was much worse than what Yasmin had described. Everyone had hate for me in their eyes; the kids were doing nothing but crying and crying. My parents had their eyes lowered as if they were ashamed of me. I tried to wish a few adults but everyone just turned and walked away, as if I were a disease.

She was tanned, had wavy brown hair but that day she looked white and her hair were in a ponytail. Her face was a peaceful and white. It was a day after she died when the funeral was taking place. They'd recently bathed her because her hair was wet. She was dressed in a beautiful suit.

I'd always loved her hair and was running my fingers through her hair but today I did not have the guts to go near her body. They'd already done her autopsy but you would never have known upon first glance.

I wanted to touch her lips, touch her hands, stroke her face but I could not. She was not there, though I was scared. Probably her body was very cold because it'd been refrigerated.

My Sarah did not look like she was sleeping. She did not look like herself at all. It was like I was looking at someone who could have been related to her but certainly not like her.

I buried my head in my hands and I could hear my breaths and tears. In my grief I thought that I was hearing sounds of life. I did, however, know that I HAD to see her dead. I would have forever thought maybe she just took off, moved somewhere, or maybe she was kidnapped. I would have had no real closure, had I not gone in there to see her. I am honestly grateful that I had to see her body one last time before she was taken away forever. I got to tell her things. I had wanted to and apologized, before she was cremated.

They took her away to the graveyard but I did not go along. I did not find it appropriate enough for a murderer to go to the victim's funeral.

"You called me?" I quietly went to my mother after they had returned. I thought she would support me because she loved me but I was wrong. In reply a hard slap came in contact with my cheek, "Look what you have done! You killed her Abraham! Who told you to go in her room and yell at her?" She spoke with hatred in her voice, "Who told you?" I asked in disbelief.

"Reyaan told us, had he not told none of us would have known!" Zara aunt yelled at me as tears kept flowing from her eyes.

"I am not going to live in the house where my daughter's murderer lives, I cannot let Zehra live here and die like my daughter." She said and walked away along with a crying Zehra and Rehman uncle.

I looked at Reyaan who had tears in his guilt filled eyes, "Sorry."

He mouthed and kept crying endlessly. Mum suddenly went upstairs and a few minutes later came out with a travel bag, "Mum?" I asked her, she raised her hand, "I am not your mother and I only have two daughters. Yasmin and Adina. I had a son but he became a murderer and…died." She threw the bag where I was standing.

"Get out of my house Abraham Khan! I will not let a murderer live in my house, get out Abraham just get out and leave us alone!" Dad yelled at me, I turned to look at my sisters but as soon as my eyes met theirs both Adina and Yasmin looked down.

"Abraham has not done anything!" Alisha tried to back me but my dad shut her up. "You please stay out of our family matters." He looked at her dead in the eye and she backed off. After this Roohi aunt also walked away while pulling Alisha with her.

"Did you not hear me?" Dad dragged me by the collar of my white shirt and pushed me out of the door with my bags, "No one needs you here Abraham! Don't ever come back!" He yelled and closed the door with a bang, leaving me to my destiny.

Chapter 16

<u>Abraham</u>

I felt a small pain at the pit of my stomach and as sentimental and overly sensitive as this sounded, I felt like... crying. "It's okay." Scarlette hugged me while rubbing my back in comfort and I cried in her hair for what seemed like forever, "Want to know more of it?" I asked while pulling away and felt her shake her head, "N-no I don't want to know." She spoke in a heavy voice and I could not help but look up at her. I looked up, my eyes glued to those addicting black olive irises looking at me.

Her face was swollen and red, she had been crying along with me, as she saw me examining her face she quickly looked away and tried to wipe her tears.

"After that day, Alisha secretly helped me and let me live at her boyfriend's house for an year. After one year of working at a bar. I collected money for the audition of Voice of UK and got selected." I sighed.

"You know what happened after that. I got into Groove at the boot camp, the band did exceptionally well with the first album itself and here I am, in the biggest band on the planet yet without a family." I forced a smile on my face and she too smiled at me.

"I wanted to ask, who was that girl with you at the club?" She looked down with tightened jaw and looked jealous, "She was Alisha."

Quickly she looked up, "Oh I thought you were flirting with her." She looked embarrassed. "She was asking me to come back home."

I casted my eyes at the floor, "And you said?" She kept her hand on mine.

"I said no. I cannot go back, the family has finally united and lives together, I cannot go back and ruin things again." I sighed and she nodded, "It is totally your will." She smiled.

"It does not hurt? I mean, I do not think I will stay away from my family for someone else."

She said innocently, "It does, it hurts a lot. But I keep things to myself so it does not hurt anyone else. Sometimes you just need to distance yourself from people. If they care, they will notice. If they do no, you know where you stand." I sighed.

"Oh and do you know the reason why I was avoiding you and never talked properly to you when you first came?" I asked her.

She shrugged, "No, I don't know. You have formed your image as a rude boy so I thought that was the reason." She gave a helpless smile.

"Look at this and you will understand," I fished out my phone and after going through the gallery I stopped at a picture and handed the phone to her.

As she examined the picture her eyes grew wide, "Oh heaven! She looks so similar to me and oh my god I have the same blue coat!" She exclaimed and looked up at me in surprise, "Who is she?" She asked with a lot of curiosity and wonder in her eyes and voice.

"She is Sarah." I smiled at her and Scarlette stared at me for a few seconds and then at Sarah's picture, "Sh-she's Sarah?" She stuttered and I nodded in reply, "Oh my God! Now I understood, you were staring creepily at me when I first joined here because you saw Sarah in me?" She asked in surprise and I nodded with a smile.

"She is so beautiful and…so similar! Only her face structure and lips are slightly different. Oh my God! She has brown wavy hair too!" She kept zooming in and zooming out the picture.

I knew this from the very first day but I never said it to her, I was scared she too would die but I could not control myself any longer.

"Will you be my girlfriend Scarlette?" I spoke all of a sudden. "Sorry?" She spoke as her head shot up at the question,

"Someday or the other both of us will have to have our other halves and I know I will not be as intimate with that girl, if she exists, as I am with you. Being intimate is not about just making love, it means knowing each other inside out and you know me completely." I blabbered.

"But Abraham my di-" I quieted her as I sealed her lips with mine. She tensed a bit but unknowingly one hand of mine went down to her waist and she seemed to get relaxed. Our lips were moving in perfect sync, the moisture of her lips were indescribable. I felt my insides melt as I kissed her, our lips parting and our tongues dancing rhythmically with one another. The kiss was gentle and completely innocent.

I pulled away breathlessly and she bit her lip before looking at me, "Okay, what was this?" She chuckled, "I don't know. But it was right, it felt right." I shrugged in reply and before I could realize she was looking at the ground with her cheeks in a deep shade of red.

Slowly she got up and started walking away, "Scar, so should I take that as a yes?" I asked her with a smirk.

She turned around, "Yeah and by the way, my name never felt so good." She blushed and went back into the room.

Chapter 17

<u>Scarlette</u>

I walked back into the room however that did not stop my heart from hammering against my ribs. I could not get my mind off our kiss, my first ever kiss, okay not first ever but my first ever kiss that felt and meant something to me, and I just came into my first ever relationship.

The kiss, it felt so real, good and right. Even though at first I was a bit surprised but his touch had put me on fire and fixed me a little, it made me let go the worries.

He kissed me and I kissed him back. I felt something in that moment that I know I will never forget. I felt happy. If there is a time in life where I need happiness, I would think back to that moment. In that moment, the moment right there. I was happy.

My fingers made their way to the nape of his neck, playing with his perfect hair. I tugged softly as I felt Abraham's teeth clamp down onto my bottom lip.

I was staring at the ground and was smiling like a fool.

Out of nowhere, I looked up to see him smiling at me, "Hi Abraham." I sigh, trying not to smile at his sight.

I felt so nervous seeing him for some reason. This feeling was very foreign to me. It felt like an eruption of butterflies exploding and caging in my ribs. I felt like my heart was rising in my throat.

I looked at him and he just looked back at me, "What are you looking at?"

I asked, running a hand through my hair, "You're so beautiful. Like rain and sunshine and the waves meeting the shore. I think you are the most beautiful thing I have ever seen." He replied with a smile that could melt anyone.

Even though we had just cried and vented our eyes out minutes before we still were happy. His eyes were red from all the crying and sleeplessness yet he looked at me, with this light in his eyes that did not let my brain get affected by outer appearance.

"What about Sarah?" I blurted out but soon regretted it, surprisingly. Instead of freaking out he grinned, "You both are almost the same." I do not know why but I did not find this comment as a compliment.

He kept relating and comparing me with Sarah; which meant he found her in me and liked the Scarlette who looks like Sarah instead of just Scarlette. However, I did not complain knowing he was very happy at that time and I can put up a war with the world rather snatching that real smile off his face.

"By the way," He spoke and made me look up, "Why did you drink so much?" He asked in concern. "Nothing great as such." I cannot tell him about Jacob or he will fight with him. I cannot let the band's reputation get in danger.

"I know you since the last seven months. I know that is not much though. Still I know that you do not touch alcohol. This was something major that made you drink." He sat down facing me and made me look in his eyes.

He has understood that trait in me that I cannot lie while looking someone in the eyes, "Look at me and say it is nothing major."

He held my hands in his.

"Promise me you will not fight or do any such thing that gives the media a juicy headline." I put my palm in front of his hand.

"Not this." He crossed his fingers over his heart, "This is our promise, okay?" He raised his eyebrows and I nodded.

"I promise I will not do any such thing." He spoke as he crossed his fingers over his heart.

"Now tell me, I am getting anxious." He held my hands again.

"I was sitting at the bar, Jacob walked o-" His face muscles tensed.

"No getting angry." I formed circles on the back of his hand with my thumb while he nodded.

"Jacob walked over to me, he asked me out, I rejected him, his manly ego got hurt so he hurled abuses at me and said no one needs me." I was looking at our hands, "I will not spare him." His grip tightened. "After that I saw you with Alisha and I thought you two were going out and I got even more depressed and chucked down three mugs of beer." I changed the order of things a bit so that he did not beat the shit out of Jacob.

"Oh okay so I am partially responsible?" He looked so cute with a guilty face, "Partially, a tiny bit." I made a small distance between my index finger and thumb to show him 'tiny' before he nodded.

"Hang on," He spoke after a bit of time, "You chucked down three mugs of beer and you are standing straight, without a hangover! Are you iron woman?" He widened his eyes in surprise.

"I tried alcohol when I was a sophomore and it was around five mugs of beer. I never got any hangover in the morning. So, maybe!" I replied laughing.

"Still, you must take care of yourself." He kissed my hand and I blushed a bit.

"And how did you come to know about Sarah? I don't think anyone knows."

He thought a bit, "Uhm you told me." I spoke nodding. "I told? What do you mean?" He had a confused look on his face. "Not the entire thing but that I remind you of Sarah." I explained, "When?" He started scratching his head.

"You remember when we got a dare to sleep next to one another?"

I raised my eyebrows and he nodded in reply, "When we were lying down then you muttered, "Sarah." and I was confused so I turned to face you. "Don't leave me Sarah." Tears started flowing from your eyes as you started moving your hands in the air. I tried to wake you up but you kept crying, unable to understand anything I stroked your head and spoke to you, "Abraham I am here, I am Sarah." As soon as I spoke that you pulled me to your chest and turned me, you snaked your arms in my waist and nuzzled your tear stained face in my neck.

"You know Sarah there is a girl, she is our stylist and her name is Scarlette Waters. She reminds me of you." After that I could not understand anything because you kept mumbling random things.

"Oh duh, I am so stupid." He smiled sheepishly, "No, it is okay, not a big deal." I tried to console him, "Of course, not a big deal. You got to sleep in my arms!" He spoke with swag and raised his collars while laughing and I guess trying to remove the awkward air.

"Yeah? I would have pushed you away but you were crying and looked too cute." I stuck my tongue out at him, "I am born cute!" He said sassily and laughed along with me.

"Anyways, I think you must take rest now. It is already two in the morning, you go to sleep." He got up from the bed and kissed my forehead this time as I blushed again. "But what about you Abraham? How will you sleep?" I asked him in concern as he wrapped his fingers around mine and helped me lay down.

"I got the most comfortable place on Earth," He turned around at my confused expression, "My lovely girl and the beautiful hospital property, I present you the beautiful and life exuberating maroon couch!" He pointed at the maroon couch kept at a little distance from the bed and clapped sarcastically while I laughed at his cuteness.

He laughed with me, "Now you sleep okay? Good night, sweet dreams, I l-" he stopped wide eyed and I almost understood what he was about to say, "I...I-'ll let you know about uh your...discharge okay? Yeah?" He spoke in a hurry and instead of waiting for my reply he laid down on the couch beside the bed.

Was he about to say 'I love you' to me? Am I that special? Am I worth it? Such questions kept floating in my brain, not letting me fall asleep, eventually I decided to shut my brain, fall asleep and rewind the events of the day in my dreams.

6 months later

"Scarlette please babe understand. This is for your good, it will make things easy for both of us. Please." Abraham walked behind me as he requested.

"No Abraham. I told you I cannot do this. I cannot be a charity case. I cannot use your money and I don't want you to pity over me." I spoke as I moved around my styling room, collecting the clothes scattered all around.

It has been thirteen months since I started working as a stylist with Groove. It is one of the best jobs in the world. My life is perfect right now. I have an exciting job. I have my own SUV that I always wanted; I have a boyfriend who loves me. And I have great best friends in Shawn, Augustus and Mark.

Though, I and Abraham are not friends with Jacob. I did not protest him and Ellie dating because I believe she is 20 now. She knows what is right and what is wrong. I am not much in terms with Oliver either either because he blamed me for Jacob's behavior at the bar that day.

Moreover, I had to lie about fainting at the club that I was dehydrated, that did not made much sense but it was Abraham's idea because I am still not ready to reveal about my health.

However, right now I am fuming with anger because Abraham was walking right behind me and convincing me to do something, I really don't want to.

The words had not rolled out of my mouth that suddenly his hands turned me and pulled me closer with his hands on my waist making all the cloths in my hand fall on the floor, "What on Earth do you think you are doing Abraham?" I was very irritated and his romancing at that moment, made no sense at all.

"Stating my point," He spoke and tightened his grip on my waist and pulled me closer. "Life at time is all about being selfish Scarlette. You are not a charity case for me, you are my girlfriend and I love you. I do not pity you. I pity myself. I cannot just let you live like this and then look at you di..,whatever it is." He always avoids using the word 'die' or talking about someone's death.

"You are my world. You are important to me. I cannot let you leave me like this. You are one of the best things that have happened to me. You have fixed me and given me the hope to stand alive here. You are my reason of living. My lifeline. It is my time to pay you back. Sorry, I may sound very selfish but I want you to be with me. I want you to get operated so that you keep your promise of being with me till infinity Scarlette. You are my infinity." He looked me in the eyes as if he could see through me.

"By the way, since when did this your money and my money come between us?" He frowned a bit. "I know it never came between us Abraham. I love you too but this is your hard earned money. I cannot just take it away from you." I cupped his face.

"Okay so you want to get your operation done with your money?" He spoke as he thought for a bit.

I nodded, "Cool, so you get the operation done-"

He kept a finger on my lips as I was about to protest, "Then from your every month's salary, that has been increased though. You give me 20,000 such that in five months you can return me the entire amount. Okay?"

He asked me and it seemed like a pretty good idea, "You are a smart boy Khan!" I said in an appreciative tone and he grinned proudly.

"But I also want interest." He said seriously, "Okay, how much?" I asked in confusion. "Lots of smiles on your face and lots of kisses for me." A warm smile crept on his face. I looked down blushing. "Will you?" He made me look up. I nodded with a smile as he engulfed me in a hug.

"Did you ever have something so beautiful that everyone wanted it?" I asked him out of nowhere. "Yup, I have you." He spoke in my hair and I couldn't help but smile at it.

"I love you Abraham." I shut my eyes tightly, feeling safe in his hug.

"I love you Scarlette." He replied as he kissed my temple.

Suddenly someone cleared their throat and we literally jumped away from one another. I turned to see Ellie and Jacob holding hands, she was smiling and Jacob was staring at me with anger. "Did we interrupt a future make out session?" Ellie wiggled her eyebrows and I blushed.

"Shut up Ellie." I put my fingers on my left eye and looked down, "Aww look at you Scar, oh God! You are red." She spoke and I shot her a glare, fighting back a smile.

"Hey brother in law! Wassup?" She looked at Abraham and made him blush with her forever teasing comments. "Can you stop that Ellie?" I glared at her and she giggled, "I just love the way he looks all red when I call him brother in law. Aww! You are so cute Abraham!" She giggled again and I rolled my eyes at her, before seeing Jacob pulls her closer to himself.

"Whoa man! Slow down there. I am just complimenting Abraham, no need to be all possessive and protective." Ellie snapped at Jacob and gave Abraham and me a hard time controlling our laughter.

We do not have anything against Jacob but I love this quality of Ellie that she never lets a man or anyone over control her. She always has her sarcastically slaying attitude that never lets anyone control her.

"Uh I think we should get going now." Abraham smiled at them, held my hand and started to walk away, "Aye Scarlette! I wanted to hang out with you guys so I took Jac with me too." She grinned excitedly but I shook my head, "Sorry Ellie but we have plans together, we will catch up next time." I made a sad face and she nodded, "Okeydokey but don't make an excuse next time please." She hugged me and we bid them adieu.

"Sorry baby but I don't like possessive people." We heard Ellie talk to Jacob and I guess give him a kiss as we walked out of the room.

"How can Ellie be so casual with Jacob after what he did?" Abraham shook his head in disbelief as we were out of their hearing area. I faced him, "You don't know?" I asked him and he shook his head, "Ellie does not know anything." His eyes widened, "Why so?" He asked.

"Because she is in love with him. And I don't want her to push him away because of me. He has changed; he is over me and likes Ellie." I told him and he nodded with a shrug, "Maybe." He sighed.

I was in deep thought as we got in the car. Suddenly Abraham's hand shaking in front of my eyes snapped me out of my thoughts. "Huh what?" I asked him, "Babe I called you around three or four times. Where is your mind? What is bothering you?" He asked me with worry written all over his face.

I could not ask him to do that directly but I wanted to ask him. I thought for a bit before smiling to myself, "What are you up to Scarlette Waters?" He asked me suspiciously and I shook my head.

"I will get the operation done if you do something for me and mind it, this is my condition." I smiled evilly at him before he face palms himself, "You and your conditions! I feel like being in a relationship with a stock market company," He raised his hands on either sides, "If you follow this xyz condition we will tell you about your profit shares, if you follow this xyz condition we will let you invest your money in our company!" He spoke in a cranky voice and I fell in a fit of laughter.

"Now may I?" I asked him as I straightened up, in reply he simply nodded, "Uhm look I've been wanting to ask you since a long time but I did-" he interrupted me, "Oh spit it already Scar!" He cried and I took a deep breath.

"I want to meet your family." I spoke quickly and looked down, I did not want to look at his face and I was already feeling guilty. "I-I would have given you whatever you wanted but t-this is something I cannot do. I feel guilty for doing all that even though Alisha told me that everyone misses me." I heard him gulp. I looked up and saw that his jaws were tightened and eyes were dark.

"I am sorry. I did not mean to hurt you." I looked down as guilt took over me and before I could realize Abraham had engulfed me in a tight hug, the one that he needed the most at such a time.

Abraham was over Sarah, though it still hurts him to think about her or any such thing because somewhere in the deepest pits of his heart. He blames himself for her death. In this time I have seen him go through pain, misery, sadness, loneliness and guilt on the 21ˢᵗ of November. The date Sarah died.

"You want to see my home? In Bradford?" His eyes lit up after he pulled away but I shook my head, "No Abraham it is fine."

"I really don't want to make you upset." I kept my hand on his and forced a smile. "No I really want to see the Khan house after so long. We won't meet them but we will just see the house from outside. Please?" He made a puppy dog face, one that I cannot resist.

This was weird. He was convincing me to go to his house. I was not ready to do so even when it should be the flip side. This is the proof of how different and out of the box, both of us are.

"You want to go?" He nodded.

"You will not feel bad and will not cry?" I pointed at him strictly. He pouted before sighing, "I will not feel bad and will not cry my girlfriend cum mother." He stuck his tongue out at me making me roll my eyes.

"So are we going?"

"Yes but keep your promise."

"I louve you my sweetie pie." The most annoying thing ever

"Of course."

Chapter 18

Scarlette

"Are you sure you want to see your house?" I asked him again after a tiring 3 hour drive that made us reach Bradford.

"Y-yeah I am sure...I guess." He bit his lip and moved his hands in the air.

"You are already feeling sad after seeing this 'Welcome to Bradford' board; I do not think you are keeping your promise." I crossed my arms.

"Nostalgic." He corrected me.

"I have spent my entire childhood here and have come here after three freaking years. How can you not expect me to be nostalgic?" He asked with shock. I just rolled my eyes at him.

Not realizing when my thoughts took over me, I fell asleep with my head resting on the window.

"Scar get up." I heard Abraham's voice after some time, confused I opened my eyes and looked around, "We are here. The Khan house."

He spoke with eyes and voice full of happiness and excitement. I got up and looked at the window to see a whit and big three storey house. It was I guess the most beautiful and simple house I had ever seen.

It had a lot of windows and one small staircase that went up to the main door. The lawn had a number of flowers and plants but the right side of the door was weirdly empty. The house was very artistic and had three cars parked. I would lie if I don't say it was quite baronial.

"Your house is so beautiful Abraham!" I exclaimed.

"I know, right? It had many flowers this side," He pointed towards the right side of the gate; "I and Adina had planted when we were little kids. I don't why they are not there anymore but they looked damn pretty." He grinned.

Suddenly a little girl came out of the main door and stared at our car, "Scarlette hide." Abraham spoke and I did not understand, "Why? Who is she?" I asked him and turned to the girl who was around eight or nine years old. "She is Zehra." He spoke and I turned towards him to see that his eyes had watered.

"I told you not to come, Abraham! You are crying!" I whispered, he looked up at me, "I am not crying because I am feeling bad but due to the memories, this place re-kindles in my head. I am crying because she has grown up so much. She was this much," He showed with his hand a girl with small height.

"She was just five years old when I saw her the last time, now she has grown up to be such a pretty eight year old girl." He wiped his eyes as he saw, who was now cycling. "Every kid must have grown up!" He exclaimed with excitement but soon looked down, "I wish I could meet them." He sighed.

"You said your aunt had shifted and Zehra is Sarah's sibling right?" I asked him in confusion, he nodded, "Alisha told me some days back that uncle got bankrupt and had to sell his house so mum asked all three of them to come back." He explained and I nodded.

The door opened again and a beautiful girl came out who scarily resembled Abraham a lot, her face cut, eyes and jawline was exactly like him. I turned to him and then to her, "W-who is she?" I stuttered, he gave a huge grin, "My baby, Yasmin. Oh God she has become so beautiful! She is nineteen now! I cannot believe this. It seems like yesterday when I held her in my arms as a little baby." He wiped his tears again.

Before going in with Zehra, she looked at our car and stared at it for a long time. She had her eyebrows furrowed and eyes in a thoughtful manner. All of a sudden shock covered her face and she quickly walked towards our car after sending Zehra inside and within seconds opened the door of the passenger's seat.

"Abr-" she turned to me and grew quite as horror was written all over her face, "S-Sarah?" she stared at me with fear evident in her eyes. "No Yasmin, I am Scarlette Waters. Abraham's-" I turned to him as if to confirm if I should girlfriend or friend, "My girlfriend." He completed my sentence.

"She looks like Sarah…a lot. This is scary!" She kept staring at me, before I awkwardly shifted in my seat; she tore her gaze away from me and turned it towards Abraham. "Look Yasmin-" Abraham looked down with guilty eyes, "It is Yasmi. Anyways, how are you Abraham?" She spoke as tears started falling from her eyes.

"Yasmin, come inside." I got out of the passenger's seat and let her in before jumping in the seat behind, as soon as she got in she hugged a surprised Abraham. "How are you? We missed you so much Abraham. It has been so long since we have seen you in reality. I missed you big brother!" They cried their eyes out and I could not help but wipe my tears at such an emotional time.

"How is everyone at home?" He asked her, she smiled, "I am doing majors in English, Zehra loves going to school like I did, Adina is getting married next year, Reyaan has married an Irish girl named Leona Horan, Zara aunt and Rehman uncle are back because they got bankrupt, Roohi aunt is a baker now, Alisha lives in London with her boyfriend at college and mum is doing fine but she misses you a lot. In fact, everyone does even uncle and aunt because now she thinks that you have had enough of staying away as a token of forgiveness." She smiled as she finished.

"What about dad? How is he?" Abraham asked and I noticed Yasmin's features tighten and eyes water, "Y-you did not know?" She stammered and Abraham shook his head, "Where is dad?" He asked with fear.

"He is dead." Yasmin looked down and tried to blink away the tears, "Two years back he was sleeping and suddenly he got a cardiac arrest and he died. Mum was so sad after you went away and she almost got depressed after dad but seeing you doing well, gives her strength." She tried to smile between tears.

"She saw me on TV?" Abraham asked happily, "Only seeing? She is the biggest Groover you will ever meet! She follows every social media account of yours. She downloads every picture, goes to every show in London and obviously sees each and every performance or interview on TV. Oh and I forgot, she gets like, 'No my son will not do this!' when rumors about you doing something wrong come out. We literally run out of the house when such thing happens because she gets massive mood swings." She laughed at the last part.

"Come inside, we never thought you would come back, we thought fame took over you." She wiped her eyes and started to get out of the car when Abraham held her hand, "N-no I don't want to go inside. Zara aunt must be there...I still cannot get that face out of my mind." Abraham shook his head and wiped the tears away.

"Hey Sar-" Both of us widened our eyes and Abraham shot a glare at her, "Sorry, um, hey Scarlette?" She tried to confirm and I nodded, "Great! Convince him please." She requested me with puppy dog eyes.

"Abraham please! If she is saying that everyone is pretty normal then what is the problem huh?" Abraham shook his head in denial. "Okay, look you think that aunt will have problems if you come home right?" She asked and he nodded, "Fine, wait then." She fished out her phone from her jacket pocket.

She dialed a number and put it on speaker, "Yasmin what are y-" He was interrupted by the other person, "Hello, where are you Yasmin?" A female voice spoke Hello from the other side. "Hi mum, I was thinking that Abraham is in town, actually I am at Starbucks and he is sitting right behind me. Mind if I bring him home?" She asked and both my and Abraham's eye balls came popping out of our eye sockets, he hit Yasmin on her arm and she hit him back.

"No." Abraham mouthed, "Yes of course dear!" Their mother exclaimed, "But what about Zara aunt?" Yasmin asked her, "She will be absolutely fine with it. She was just now showing me a picture of Abraham and some girl who looked very similar to Sarah," Both of them turned to me while stifling their laughter. "Oh okay, so should I ask him to come over?" She asked Mrs. Khan.

"Yes, come as soon as possible. I will make his favorite biryani and samosas for him!" She squealed with happiness, "Mum chill we're almost there. Bye, take care." As soon as she disconnected the call she turned to Abraham, "Mum is making samosas! After so long! Thank you Abraham." Her mouth watered and both of us laughed.

"Err...what are samosas and biryani?" I asked in a clueless way, "Oh samosas are a triangular kind of pastry with spicy kind of potatoes or cottage cheese filled inside and it is spicy and tastes lovely. Really love it and biryani is fried or baked chicken along with scented and colored rice. Actually, most of Indian food is spicy and the Nan bread balances it. You'll love it!" Yasmin described and it really sounded yummy.

"Sounds tasty!" I beamed at them and she nodded, "Tastier than tasty." Their mouths watered again, "Oh my God! You two are so in love with biryani and samosas!" I laughed and they nodded again with big grins on their faces.

"I really was missing you all so much and I was wishing to come home but I did not have the guts. Thank you so much to Scarlette, she pushed me forward and I decided to come over to show her the house form outside. I am so happy! I love you baby." He turned back and kissed me when Yasmin suddenly cleared her throat.

"So you have already exchanged the 'I love yous' huh!" She wiggled her eyebrows before receiving a playful hit from Abraham, "When did you grow up so much?" He asked and she smiled, "When you got such a beautiful girlfriend!" She replied and caused both of us to blush.

"How did you both get to the I love you point? I mean when did you say it?" She asked me and I blushed a little again, "He said I love you on my birthday. On the 23rd of July last year." I informed her and she widened her eyes, "Hey that is my birthday too!" She squealed and we both hugged in happiness as Abraham rolled his eyes.

"Can we go in now?" He asked impatiently and she nodded before getting out of the car with us. Unsure of what to do I held Abraham's hand and followed in quietly, she rang the bell and I could feel his palms sweating, I gave him a quick peck on his cheek and he turned to me while looking in my eyes before sound of a door made us both look straight.

"Abraham my baby!" A lady whom I assumed to be Mrs. Khan squealed and engulfed him in a tight hug while shutting her eyes tightly to not let the tears flow out, she was in her mid-forties I suppose but was very smart and elegant looking, she wore white pants and blue shirt, she had brown straight hair and it did not take me much time to register that both Abraham and Yasmin had inherited her eyes, cheekbones and face cut.

She pulled away, "Oh sweetheart, you must be his girlfriend?" She asked me and I nodded with a smile, "Yes ma'am, Scarlette Waters." I put my hand in front and she shook her head, "Oh no dear call me Noor." She said as she engulfed me in a hug too which I gladly accepted.

"Can we get in mum?" Yasmin asked impatiently and Noor pulled away before letting us in to the house that welcomed us with smell of biryani and samosas, I guess. "Smells like heaven." Abraham spoke as he sniffed in the air with eyes closed as if he was in heaven. I followed him closely behind because this was his house and I was very nervous.

"Hello Abraham, how are you?" Another lady entered the room, she was similar to Mrs. Khan but she had black curly hair and was dark in complexion, "I am good aunt, what about you?" Abraham spoke awkwardly, "Oh my God! You have grown up so much!" She said and hugged him after which he smiled.

She looked at me and then looked at the floor, I could see tears fall down on the floor, "Zara ma'am, please control yourself. You must not cry, Sarah would not like it if she saw her mother cry." I said as I could not control myself and hugged her. Soon she looked up with a smile, wiped her tears and pulled away, "Hello Zara ma'am, I am Scarlette Waters, Abraham's girlfriend." I smiled to her and she nodded, "I know, I saw that on the internet some time back. You look very similar to my daughter. I am sorry I got emotional sweetheart." I nodded in reply.

"Adina! Reyaan! Leona! Alisha! Zehra! Come downstairs!" Mrs. Khan yelled looking at the stairs behind her and I felt Abraham tense up at the mention of Reyaan's name. He was looking at the floor with tightened jaw and breath rapid, "Abraham please calm down. Don't get angry." I whispered to him and he looked at me before nodding.

As we looked up a girl of our age walked down, she was a bit smooth around the corners and had chubby cheeks, she carried herself with confidence in a black dress and I noticed she was wearing an engagement ring which by Yasmin's information made me assume was Adina, Abraham's older sister. Adina raised her eyebrows at Abraham's sight, she seemed confused and shocked.

Followed by her was a familiar face, Alisha Khan. She grinned happily at our sight; she was the only person in the Khan clan Abraham was in contact with. She was more of a tomboy; she was wearing blue denims with black crop top and brown leather jacket. She was holding hands with Zehra who was in the same red frock.

After Alisha and Zehra entered a tall, tanned boy with short curly hair, he seemed of our age group, his face was round and eyes were dark green, he was wearing a wedding ring. With the look of fear and shock on his face I assumed him to be Reyaan. He looked nice in a dark grey t-shirt and light grey trousers.

A young blonde followed closely behind him, she was very fair and blue eyed, she looked beautiful in a green long top and skin tight black jeans. She also was wearing a wedding ring which made it pretty sure that she was Reyaan's wife Leona.

"Abraham! How nice to see you after so long!" Adina walked quickly and hugged him, "And you beautiful lady?" She asked me with a big grin, "I am Scarlette Waters." I introduced myself and she nodded with raised eyebrows, "Abraham's girlfriend." She said cheekily and it did not take me too long to grow red.

"Hi dude!" Alisha came over and hugged both of us after Adina left me after a hug, "You look good Scarlette." She smiled at me, "Thank you Alisha." I grinned at her. "How do you know each other when you met for the first time?" Zara aunt furrowed her eyebrows at us and all three of us face palmed in our heads.

"I have seen her on the internet! Abraham Khan's girlfriend! Come on aunt." Alisha managed to lie but aunt was still not the one to keep quiet, "Then how does she know you?" She asked Alisha, "Abraham told me. I have seen all of you, in pictures." I too managed a swift escape and she nodded before Abraham shot a glare at both of us.

"Abraham!" Zehra ran to him and hugged his feet joyfully, "Hello Zehra! How have you been?" He asked her, "I am good.

How are you?" She asked cutely, "I am very good now." He smiled.

"Are you his wife?" She asked me and both of us looked at each other wide eyed before I kneeled down, "No Zehra, I am his girlfriend Scarlette." I replied, she nodded, "You are so pretty! Like Sarah was!" She exclaimed happily and everyone looked very uncomfortable and awkward, "No dear, you are the prettiest!" I pecked her cheek and she giggled as I got up.

"Hey man." Reyaan spoke awkwardly as he looked at the floor, "Hi Reyaan, come on, you don't meet a brother like this, do you?" Abraham replied and took him by surprise by hugging him. "I forgot you don't do things what brothers do!" Abraham spoke sarcastically while pulling away; embarrassing Reyaan before I nudged his ribs, "No." I mouthed.

"Hello Reyaan." I smiled and put my hand out sweetly, "Oh hi Scarlette." He shook hands with me and quickly pulled it away. "Uhm, is it wrong that I don't know any of them?" Leona asked in a thick Irish accent unsurely.

"No, it is completely fine young lady." Abraham smiled at her, "Even I don't know you. Actually, who does?" He spoke in a rude manner and I nudged his ribs again. "He is Abraham Khan from Groove and I am Scarlette Waters his stylist and girlfriend." I smiled sweetly at her.

"And who are you?" Abraham asked her, sensing the tension I looked at Reyaan and he stepped in, "She is my wife Leona Khan." He turned to her, "Lee this is my elder brother and Adina and Yasmin's sibling Abraham. She is his girlfriend Sar-Scarlette Waters." He gulped at his mistake.

Each of them was extremely good looking. I was very much intimidated by Leona and Adina.

"Can I go and see my room?" Abraham asked Mrs. Khan excitedly, she nodded, "It is still there? Untouched?" He asked him and she nodded again with a smile. "The keys to your and Sarah's rooms." Mrs. Khan said while handing him a set of keys that had its 'Khan rooms' key ring flashing on it. As he moved ahead he held my hand and turned to me, "Come, let us show you my and Sarah's room." He smiled and I walked with him.

We first went to Sarah's room; I assumed this as he told me that her room was downstairs. On reaching, he handed me the keys, "The end of my life's first chapter started from this lock, I want the reason of my life's second and most important chapter to open the old one." He pecked my hand and smiled. I picked the cold steel lock, inserted the 'S' engraved key and twisted it to reveal a white and lemon colored room.

I walked in carefully to see a floor length closed window with white curtains, the room was not very clean because of being closed for the last three years but it was quite big. There was a small double bed placed in the middle with sheet and pillow covers that might have been white then but were covered with dust, next to the bed was a bed side table with a circle lamp, the thing that caught my eye in the room was that the bed sheet was unmade, dirty and next to the bed was a switched off electric socket that had a charger plugged in, this revealed that only the blood stains were cleaned but other than that the room was literally untouched.

The other side of the bed had a flower vase with rotten orchids; it had a lemon colored revolving plastic chair that was covered under deep layers of dust. The lemon and white walls had pictures of Sarah and Abraham or Sarah and everyone else hanged. I almost laughed at a picture of Abraham and Sarah as little kids; he was this chubby and grumpy kid that everyone loved to pull cheeks of.

There was a wooden wardrobe near the bed, there were scratches of age and ignorance on the wood of the wardrobe, the steel handle had rusted and there was a key that flashed a Jonas Brothers key ring hanging to the keyhole. I twisted it to reveal neatly stacked clothes and accessories that I did not dare to touch; these things still belonged to Sarah.

Next to the wardrobe was a black television. There was a small wooden study table kept close to the wardrobe a little ahead of the bed, it had a few textbooks stacked neatly on one corner while the other corner had a red pencil case kept. There was a school bag kept on the chair in front of the table under a lot of dust.

On the lemon and white colored walls in front of the bed and above the study table were slightly torn posters of Zac Efron and Jonas Brothers revealing their handsome faces under layers of dust. The posters made it clear that Sarah too had the similar music taste as I have; she too was a fan of Jonas Brothers and Zac Efron like me. How similar can two people who have never met be?

I turned to open another door that was the bathroom. It was divided in two parts by a not so high wall, one part had the toilet seat and a small wash basin while the other part had a bath tub, a washing basin and just behind the wall of the bathroom seat was a Jacuzzi. There was a big in breadth mirror above the washing basin that was next to the bath tub.

There were small tubes shaped LEDs on the either sides of the mirror and some circle shaped above the tub other than the CFLs. The white marble had become brown and the expired lotions and shampoos still lay near the tub.

I turned to see Abraham but he was not in the bathroom, I walked back into the room to see him touching his and Sarah's picture. "I miss you Sarah, I am sorry." He whispered to himself before I cleared my throat and he turned around, startled. "I-I am sorry I-" I shook my head, "It's okay. Won't go in?" I tried to change the topic.

He shook his head in denial, "I cannot go there…I-I will not able to see the bathroom again." He stuttered and I nodded because I did not want to force him.

After closing the bathroom door, the room door and locking it we went upstairs and he was very excited and happy to see his room after so long. Turning right from the staircase there were a number of doors and rooms, this house was nothing less than a mansion.

He handed me the keys and stood in front of a brown door that had a lock on it, I opened it with a key that had 'A' engraved on it to reveal a blue and white room.

There was a slanting window on the roof and a textured wall. There was a double bed placed right in the middle with striped white and grey unmade bed sheet and pillow covers of the same kind. On the either side of the bed were wooden bedside tables that had lamps and things like alarm clock, charger and family pictures placed since the last three years. On the wall behind the bed were three framed jerseys signed by David Bekham, Cristiano Ronaldo and Lionel Messi hanging. The walls boasted posters of The Beatles, Manchester United and Nirvana. Next to bed was a guitar kept parallel to the wall.

A football and some cigarette butts were lying shabbily in the room. It was a typical teenager boy's room, the dirty one with lots of posters and football merchandise. There was a wooden wardrobe with posters of Manchester United on it, like Sarah's his cupboard too had the keys dangling but I did not open it because he was standing right behind me. There were only three pictures of non-famous people i.e. his family in the room. One was a family picture kept on a bed side table, other was a picture of him and Sarah on the other table, the third was a big picture of Mrs. Khan, his sisters and him.

There was a small study table on one corner with textbooks scattered all over it and on the surface was scribbled with compass or a sharp object, 'Sarah <3 Abraham." I looked away awkwardly and turned around to find him looking around at everything in admiration. "These posters, these jerseys, everything is here!" He exclaimed and stroked the posters while I smiled at his happiness.

To the other side was a black television that had two bean bags in front of it and around the bean bags a number of video game CDs, art books and comic books.

After quite a while of looking around his room and cupboard we went downstairs to the others. "The rooms are still the same mum!" He exclaimed like a little kid, "When Sarah died, in anger we also sent you away from us. So, I decided if Sarah's room is kept the same then yours too much be kept untouched." She smiled dotingly and hugged him again.

All through the day we had delicious lunch made by Mrs. Khan along with a great laugh. I must say she is a great cook and I have fallen in love with samosas and biryani, she is a pro at it. The Khan family had very readily accepted me and Abraham, at the table there was even a serious time when Mrs. Khan started telling Abraham about his father Yaser Khan but seeing the sadness on everyone's faces she shook it off. I noticed Reyaan tensed all through the time because I guess he was nervous that Abraham would tell everyone about their past but Abraham did not. I guess he had forgiven Reyaan.

Suddenly, Abraham stood up, "We have to leave now." Mrs. Khan held his hand, "Oh Abraham please stay here for at least a fortnight! You have come after three long years." She requested him. He kept his hand on hers, "It is already seven and it takes three hours to reach London. Moreover, a drive so late with a girl is not a very safe thing." She nodded understanding the situation.

He hugged everyone including Reyaan and Leona. Suddenly, Yasmin and Alisha pulled me away from everyone, "Abraham loves you the most. He's got a big heart. Don't ever leave him!" Yasmin said to me. "Huh? I don't think he is over Sarah yet." I shrugged at her; she smiled and replied "Scarlette! He is my brother I know him. I have seen the look in his eyes when he sees you, the sparkle when you blush. You are the first girl that brings the light in his eyes. Trust me! He loves you, Sarah is his past." Alisha smiled and held my hand.

"I too love him Alisha. I promise I'll never leave him." I blushed for the hundredth time, "That's like my girl!" She replied hugging me. "Scarlette! Abraham is waiting outside." Adina tapped my shoulder and said smiling. "I'm there." I hugged Yasmin and Alisha and ran off to the gate. We bid them adieu and left as he put the car in ignition.

"It is great you are going along well with my mother and sisters." Abraham said smirking at me. "They're such sweet people specially Aunt and Alisha!" I grinned at him, "That's great!" He said in a sarcastic tone and I decided to I ignore the sarcasm.

"By the way you were very rude to Reyaan and Leona!" I scolded him, "Yeah right! Reyaan did such a great thing right?" He snorted. "I understand but what has Leona done? She is just Reyaan's wife, she is innocent and so you must not be rude to her Abraham. Please behave yourself." I said strictly, "Okay mom." He chuckled, pecked my cheek and made me roll my eyes.

Chapter 19

Scarlette

"Ellie!" I called Ellie as I entered our house after a long day of shopping with May. Three weeks have passed since I and Abraham visited his place and he has been the happiest person on the planet ever since then. I am seriously very happy and grateful to God for him; he finally found happiness at the same place where he misplaced it.

"Ellie?" I called again but did not get any reply. I took the two shopping bags for her and walked to her room. Before I could knock I noticed the sound of someone's crying. Without knocking I barged into the room only to find Ellie as a heap of tears on the floor, she never cried so much and here she was lying on the floor with tears flooding in her eyes.

"Ellie oh my God! What happened to you?" I rushed to her side and pulled her in my lap, "Ellie baby get up! Tell me dear what happened?" I pulled her up and she just hugged me tightly and cried in my hair. "He broke my heart Scarlette." She spoke between her tears, "Who broke your heart? Who did what?" I stroked her hair.

She pulled away and I examined her features, her hands were shivering, her eyes and nose was red, all her liner was running down and her hair was in a mess. "Jacob." She broke down again, "What did he do?" I held her hand in mine and made her sit on her knees in front of me.

Ellie was never the kind of girl who would cry over a boy or a break up, she was strong and straightforward. She had fallen in love for the first time and got her heart broken, "He does not love me back Scarlette." She buried her face in her hands, "It is okay Ellie. It is not important that the person you love always loves you back. Love is not perfect, that is the most perfect thing about love and it doesn't exist until it does baby girl." I held her face but she shook her head.

I could see my little Ellie again; the one scared of bad dreams and darkness which was lost somewhere in the process of growing up.

"That is the problem Scarlette, if he would have not loved me I would have understood but he used me. He wanted the world for him but I just wanted to be his, is it too much to ask for love? I wanted to be *the one* but for him I was always, the other one. I did not believe in love until today, the day my heart got broken by my first love." She spoke as tears kept staining her cheeks.

"Tell me clearly Ellie, what happened? How did he use you and what did he do?" I asked her after wiping her tears away, "He was never in love with me; he used me as a weapon to make you jealous." She spoke and took me by shock. "He thinks you are in love with him but have not realized it, so he thought that if he dates your sister you will get jealous and dump Abraham to date him." She hugged me again and the only question in my mind was nothing but- How could Jacob fall so low?

"Who told you this and when?" I asked her, she hiccupped, "I heard him talking to Oliver. He discussed this, with him this morning. I feel like shit Scarlette, it was so good when I was rude, how stupid of me to fall for him charm and addictive kisses!" She face palmed her, after pulling away.

"I don't think I will be able to make it to the party today, you go and return the dresses." She wiped her tears and got up, "You will come. It is May's birthday party; we are not going to let her down just because of Jacob and Oliver. You will be staying with me and Abraham okay?" I asked her and she nodded sadly.

In the evening

The doorbell rang at 7 as I finished putting my thick mascara. I was wearing a red dress ending just above my knees with black leather jacket and black leather boots. For a change of look I had done the winged eyeliner with mascara and bright red lip color. I walked to the door before checking my look in the mirror.

I opened the door to find a Abraham in a plain white shirt, maroon tie and khaki pants with black shoes. Though he did not overdo anything, he still looked sexier than ever, without exchanging words both of us eyed the other.

"Someone is looking gorgeous!" He whistled and I blushed and accepted his hug gladly.

"Thank you. You don't look bad either." I replied and he raised his eyebrows before rolling his eyes.

"How and where is Ellie? You told me about what Jacob did, how could he stoop so low?" He spoke in anger and disbelief as we got in and I closed the door.

"I know, right? You should have seen Ellie's condition when I reached home today. My God she was so sad. She had fallen in love for the first time and got such a massive heartbreak." I looked down at the floor while shaking my head.

Seeing me like that, Abraham put his arm around me, "You know I do not like when my baby girl is sad. Why is she not smiling her million dollar smile? We will handle Jacob and make Ellie smile, I promise." He kissed my cheek before I looked up at him and pecked his lips.

"I will go and check on Ellie until then you sit in my room. Should I get you coffee? Your hands are chilling." I said as I touched his hands, "I want to get warm some other way." He spoke with a cheeky grin and I face palmed myself before going red.

"You are gross, Abraham."

"You cannot stop smiling Scarlette." He wiggled his eyebrows and I chose to avoid him by going to Ellie's room.

"Ellie, can I come in?" I asked at the door to receive an hmm. "Hey angel, what are you we-" My eyes went wide at what I saw, "Why are you moving around in your oversized t-shirt and hot pants Ellie?" I exclaimed at her as she stood in front of me in minions t-shirt, messy bun and denim hot pants. "I don't want to go Scarlette." She said as she went and sat down on her bed while licking Nutella off a spoon.

"Why?" I crossed my arms on my chest, "Because...m-my hair is greasy." She looked at everywhere but where I was standing and I already understood she was lying. "Ellie please, you are not going because of Jacob." She nodded and looked down at the floor.

"Ellie, try to understand, you will be with us and we will not let him mess with you. Moreover, you have to show him what he lost. Please come or I am also not going and Abraham is also not going, we will be sitting here on your head." She chuckled and nodded.

"Fine, but you decide what I should wear." She said as she got up and opened her wardrobe; Ellie's wardrobe was something to die for. She was one of the most stylish kids in school and in the colony, her clothes were neither too seductive nor too plain, they were in between and looked perfect.

"You choose anything Ellie; all your dresses are great." I shrugged but she shook her head side to side, "I am in no mood of selecting dresses. You select any of it, give it to me, I will put it on and then do my makeup and hair." She was genuinely not in a mood.

I went through her wardrobe and selected the perfect dress and handed it to her. She went to the bathroom and after a couple of minutes walked out looking absolutely sexy, the dress was a sleeveless black lace dress ending on her mid thighs with black leather boots till a little above the ankle. I curled her hair which were not greasy in big curls and left it, open on one side. For the makeup I did the smoky eye look with bright red lip color and Y contour.

"Tada!" I showed her the mirror and she widened her eyes, "Oh my God my talented stylist!" She clapped and I giggled. "It has been one hour thirty minutes since I am here and have not even got a kiss! Is this how you treat your guest?" Abraham shouted from my room and we giggled before walking there and opening the door.

"Yes, this is how I treat guests. I do not kiss them!" I said sassily but he did not reply instead he eyed Ellie, "You look so... different and good!" He said approvingly, "Credit to the sexy stylist for convincing me to get ready and doing my make up." She pointed towards me and both of them clapped.

We went down from the lift to his car after locking the house. "Want Starbucks?" He asked before slowing the speed near a Starbucks but we shook our head, "It is already 8:45, I don't want to go late at May's party." He nodded before shrugging and quickening the pace. After a fifteen minute drive we reached at May's farmhouse which was quite big.

However, before that we had to face the paparazzi, "I cannot face their questions." Ellie gulped and shook her head. "Abraham Khan has a solution to everything Ellie John Waters!" He said as if he were some heavenly saint. "Please enlighten us Saint

Abraham Khan!" I said sarcastically and he nodded before putting his hands in his pocket.

He took out an mp3 player, "Put it in your ear and play some nice Justin Beiber or Taylor Swift song on full volume." We clapped at the brilliant idea, "And what if one of them pulls it out of my ear? They are not so sweet." Ellie stated, "They will not, my bodyguards are here. They will be on either sides of you both and make sure no one touches you." He smiled at us and we nodded as Ellie put the mp3 player with *I Knew You Were Trouble by Taylor Swift.*

As we got out we saw only two guards and I put them around Ellie, I started to walk with my head down but someone touched my hand before pulling it away. I turned around to see Abraham staring at a paparazzi, "No dude, you do not touch her." He spoke through gritted teeth and before he would get in a fight I held his hand and shook my head side by side after which he moved next to me protectively.

We quickly walked in, "Happy birthday Mayu." Abraham hugged her and we called her by her nickname, "Thank you guys." She grinned happily, "Your present is in your cabin, get it tomorrow morning." He told her and she nodded excitedly.

"Hey." Abraham said as we walked to the boys and Ellie's grip on my hand tightened as Jacob came into sight, suddenly she left my hand, "Hey guys." She chirped and hugged everyone except Jacob and just eyed him with disgust and I understood she did it on purpose. Abraham looked at me from the corner of his eyes and I smirked before shrugging.

He was standing there looking at us in a white t-shirt, bluish grey jacket and black jeans. His hair was in perfect messy curls and shoes were black.

"Can I dance with the beautiful lady here?" Someone said and we turned around to see a very popular Hollywood star Ansel Mendes, "Sorry?" Ellie asked him, "Can I have a dance with you? The next number is a romantic one." He asked as he held his hand out which Ellie gladly accepted.

"She is my girlfriend." Jacob spoke for the first time the entire evening through gritted teeth, I could see tears well up in her eyes but she blinked them away, "You should have thought that before using me as a weapon." She eyed him again before turning away with Ansel.

Jacob's fists balled up and anger was evident in his eyes with his rapid breath, "There is no use of getting angry Jacob, all of us know you got nothing in your heart for Ellie and you used her to make me jeal-" I was interrupted by the anger in his eyes, "When you do not know then do not speak! I am in love with her," He pointed where Ellie stood with Ansel on the dance floor. All our eyes were widened except Oliver, "Today in the morning when she barged in the room crying that was when Jacob said that this *was* his plan and now he actually loves her more than she does." Oliver explained us.

"I don't know if you guys are saying the truth or not, after certain things I don't think I can believe you." I shook my head in denial. He nodded, "Ellie and I complete seven months tomorrow, look what I got for her day before yesterday." He said and pulled up the right sleeve of his jacket to show a tattoo, "I got this for her." He said and on closer inspection it read, 'Ellie - Jacob.' On an infinity symbol.

"If I was not in love with her and not serious for her why would I get a tattoo to keep a memory of us forever?" He asked us and this made me believe that he was actually telling the truth.

"I know I used to say that I loved Scarlette but I did not, I was just attracted to her and had a crush on her. But Ellie is different, she is perfect and beautiful, she has accepted me the way I am and has turned a deaf ear on all past stories or rumors. She accepted me and did not ask me to change even after knowing that I tried to rape her sister. She is the girl I had always wanted and I pray to God daily…That I get to marry her one day." He closed his eyes tightly and gulped hard, as if controlling himself.

Before I could reply there was an announcement, "All the couples out there, come up on the stage with your partner, a slow song for all to dance on." May's voice travelled through the speakers.

All the boys except Jacob held their girl's hand and went on the dance floor but as we reached we saw Ellie dancing with Ansel, his one arm on her waist whilst the other intertwined with hers. She was a bit shorter and so had her head on his chest, we quietly went and started dancing together.

I was looking into Abraham's eyes, the eyes that had stars of a millions of galaxies and the love of gazillion cupids. How can God be so cruel to such a pure person like him? I kissed him and I could see how surprised he was but he kissed me back.

"Leave me Jacob!" Ellie's voice pulled us apart, "You cannot dance with him." Jacob spoke to her, "Oh and why? I can dance with anyone I want Jacob. You don't control my life... anymore." Tears almost found their way out of her eyes.

"I hate you Jacob, you used me. You never loved me." She said controlling the tears that were threating to spill from her eyes. "I love you Ellie." He too was trying to hide the water in his eyes, "Can I know wha-" Ansel was interrupted by Oliver who pulled him away while talking to him.

"No you don't Jacob. You love my sister, not me." She said pointing towards me and I was suddenly feeling very guilty for breaking them up. "If I love Scarlette then why will I get your and my name tattooed? I would get her and my name, right?" Her eyes widened in confusion and I could see her anger flying right out of the window, if there was any window here.

"What do you mean?" She asked him and he pulled his sleeve after saying, "This was supposed to be shown tomorrow, on our first anniversary but...it is the same thing." He showed her the tattoo and she did not reply at first.

She traced it carefully and tried to control her tears from bursting, she looked up at him with a smile playing on her lips and happy tears engulfing her eyes. "I love you Ellie John Waters." Jacob spoke and held her hands, "I love you too Jacob Edward San Tiago." She said and jumped into his arms whilst ruining her eye makeup.

She kept her one hand on his shoulder and the other one gripped the collar, "If you ever even *try* to hurt me again Jacob San Tiago, I am going to kill myself." She threatened him,

"And I will kill myself after that because you are my infinity."
He said kissing her and I could not help but clap at the cute
scene in front of me.

"Why didn't you call me then?" She asked him, "I thought
if I call you then you would jump out of the phone, stab me
a gazillion time and then ask my dead body that why had I
called. I am scared of you babe!" He caused all of us to laugh.

The next song too was a romantic one; we danced next to Jacob
and Ellie who were happier than anything in the world. She
never stopped smiling and he never stopped kissing her, they
were relationship goals.

Chapter 20

3 years later

It's been four and a half years since Abraham and I have started dating. He got me operated two years back and it was successful. Now I may die a natural death. The Khans have gladly accepted us, he has forgiven Jacob and Reyaan. Ellie and Jacob are going strong and I couldn't have been any less proud of them. Ellie and I have moved in with our respective boyfriends but right now we are all sitting at Shawn and Oliver's house.

"Shawn William Cordan! Save your ass because I am going to kick it bad." I yelled at the top of my voice as I chased Shawn all through the house. "Scarlette! Calm down." Abraham held my hand as Shawn ran upstairs. "Calm down? He uploaded our picture, in the bed, he's an asshole." I replied to which Shawn yelled, "Oh come on Scarlette Waters! You guys were dressed, just in the same blankets!" To this Abraham left me and cracked up with the other boys.

"Shawn trust me if I co-" I stopped mid-sentence and smirked evilly. "Scar! What's wrong?" He asked me suspiciously. "Power puff girls get Shawn's ass!" I yelled as Jessica and Jennifer held Shawn from behind and laughed. To the name given in a second's thought, the boys rolled on the floor and laughed with Isabella who had just joined the drama.

Isabella Nelson was Mark's girlfriend of two years and she was a very sweet girl. She was a singer in a girl band called Little Magic and her voice was nothing but pure bliss. Isabella was the type of girl who was cheeky, naughty, sarcastic but also very genuine. She and Mark were the perfect couple because both of them had their first love as food.

"Come get him Scarlette!" Jennifer yelled. As I was about to reach him suddenly someone tickled them which made them leave Shawn. I turned to see who it was, to my shock, it was Ellie. Seeing the battlefield pause, he ran into the room behind them and locked the door.

"Ellie Waters! You are my sister!" I gasped at her. "Aww how sweet of you elder sister! Thank you for the update Scarlette Waters." She batted her eyelashes and I just raised my eyebrows at her sassy comment. "Well, own sister on one side and boyfriend's best friend one the other side." She said and blew a kiss towards Jacob who returned it. These little cheese balls! I could not help but roll my eyes over their never pausing kisses and hugs.

I and Ellie along with Jessica and Jennifer went down towards the boys who were now talking normally except Isabella and Mark who were still laughing at what happened. "You can come out Shawn Cordan! I'm just kidding! I will not kick your valuably precious ass!" I said sarcastically calling Shawn. "I know you still love me!" He said as he cheerfully came down and I rolled my eyes for the hundredth time.

I was sitting next to Abraham and all of us were talking about what should we do on the Valentine's day weekend when someone knocked at the door, "Who's it?" Oliver asked, "Sir I'm David." Said David, the gateman, "Come in." Shawn replied. "Good Morning," He wished us, "Madam your parcel." He handed me a parcel and excused himself. I turned around the plane envelope and looked up at the others who were already staring at it.

Ellie snatched it, opened the pink and white card and read it, suddenly she screamed, "Ellie! What's wrong?" Jacob asked, "Ashley is getting married!" She squealed to which I also screamed. The others stared at us with confused eyes, "Oh!" Ellie said, "Sorry. Actually Ashley is our cousin, she is of the same age and she is getting married. The first marriage of our generation!" She jumped. "Read it loud." I shook her.

She cleared her throat and read, "Become a treasured part of our journey together in which we, Ashley Marie Sholes and Brent Thomas Patrick will be united as Mr. and Mrs. Brent Patrick. With the blessings of our parents Mr. Raymond C. Sholes and Mrs. Liana R. Sholes (The bride) and Mr. Thomas J. Patrick and Mrs. Caroline T. Patrick (The groom) we request the honor of your presence at our marriage ceremony, on Saturday, the fourteenth of February at ten o'clock in the morning. St. Joseph's Church, London, United Kingdom is the place where two hearts will now be one."

"Oh my God! Ashley! We used to play together as kids, damn! We've grown up, like, we are approximate 26 year old big boys and girls." Ellie said in excitement. "Holy shit!" I exclaimed, "What happened?" she asked me in worry. "14 Feb! A week to go! We have to go shopping!" I yelled in happiness. "Right! But first let's video call Ashley-" I turned to the others who were left out, "You guys also join, after all we are one big family." I beamed. They quickly came in front of the laptop.

"Hiiii!" Ashley screamed from the screen, "Hey bitch." I and Ellie said together. "You are getting married? Brent? Your boyfriend?" I asked her, she blushed and nodded, "Oh my God! You guys were dating since the last 5 years and he proposed you?" I said happily.

Abraham

Scarlette and Ellie are so happy hearing about their sister's wedding, they are literally jumping right now. "Yes." Ashley answered. "Oooh! Look at the bride go red!" Ellie teased her, "Heaven! You are so lucky! It was always my dream that my future husband proposes me for marriage!" Scarlette said on the verge of jumping again. "Abraham will" her sister smiled teasingly, "Right Abraham?" She asked me and I could not hide the red color of my cheeks.

"I never told you about us. How do you know?" Scarlette asked her with furrowed eyebrows. "Come on! The world knows! You are a stylist for Groove and your boyfriend is a singer in the same and biggest boy band on earth!" She elaborated with hands flying in the air.

"Meet everyone-" Scarlette turned the screen towards us, "I know each and every one of them!" Ashley said, "How?" Ellie asked. "Paparazzi and Media." We nodded understanding the situation, paparazzi and media never leave us alone, obviously people know us.

"Tell me who they are." Ellie said. "You are Ellie, Jacob San Tiago, Shawn Cordan, Jennifer Cullen, Jessica Smith, Oliver Edwards, Mark Merchant, Isabella Nelson, Scarlette and Abraham Khan!" She said in the order in which we were sitting. "You know all of us?" Jessica asked in shock. "Yes Jessica!" she smiled.

A boy joined Ashley in the conversation; he was a smart boy in a grey hoodie and black jeans, "Hello I am the groom Brent Patrick! All you guys have to come to our wedding okay? No excuses. I have to meet you all." He invited us. "Sure we will!" Ellie said in excitement. "I have to go, too many preparations! It was great talking to you people, wishing to meet soon, love you all, bye!" They waved at us. "Bye!" We waved back.

"Never realized Paparazzi made us so popular!" Jessica said.

"Exactly the same thing I was thinking!" Oliver said.

"Girls! It's Friday! We have got a Saturday plan!" Ellie beamed. "Oh yes! We will go shopping!" Isabella said in her forever happy and excited mood. "You are selecting my clothes." Isabella said to Scarlette, "I am a stylist." she replied. The girls started to talk about their wedding dresses when Shawn butted in, "What about us?" Pointing towards him and us.

"We will miss you all." Jacob said.

"A lot!" I said.

"We will be lonely!" Oliver said.

"A lot!" Mark said.

"Oh really?" Ell asked us,

"Yes." We nodded innocently with pouts.

"We will not go without you guys-" Scarlette was interrupted by us dancing and the girls staring at her, "Who will pay for our dresses then?" She completed the sentence. Now it was our turn to stare at her and the girls to dance.

"But-" Jacob spoke up, "You will not?" Ellie asked "innocently" raising her eyebrows at Jacob. "Uh, um, we will." He mumbled.

Next Day At the mall

Scarlette and I along with Ellie, Jessica, Jennifer, Isabella, Jacob, Shawn, Oliver and Mark have come for shopping. While the girls are busy getting dresses it is pretty clear that we boys are not enjoying the shopping session. "How do I look?" Ellie asked Jacob who was busy in his phone, coming out of the changing room, wearing a purple sleeveless gown. "You look stunning." Jacob replied looking up from his phone, "Thank you. I am surely buying this." She said and went inside.

"This looks good?" Jessica asked Oliver, doubtfully. "I think that yellow one will look prettier." He said pointing at a yellow dress with quarter sleeves. "I think the same." She said and went towards the dress to try it out. Oliver and Jessica are the most mature couple amongst us, all of our silly chees balls while these two are like our parents.

"Mark! Mark!" Isabella called Mark. "Yes." He went towards her, "Babe please! Help me. This is a dark color for a wedding right?" She asked him. "Yes! Navy blue for a wedding, I don't think so is a good idea." He replied looking her up and down. "Thank you! You and I are so same" She squealed and left Mark who whined and went to the food joint.

"This is so costly! Shawn will buy it for me if I told him I like it. I better go with the red one." Jennifer murmured to herself. "Buy it Jenny!" Shawn said that caused Jennifer to jump back, "Uh, S-Shawn! Hi. You scared me!" She said, "Buy the dress." He said to her, "No not at all! I like the red one." She faked a smile, "Jenny I know you! You love blue and not red. Take it as a Valentine's Day gift from me okay?" He said, she nodded happily before hugging him.

I was looking around at everyone who was busy in helping their girlfriend or selecting the dresses for them.

Scarlette

"This or this?" I asked Abraham, showing him a Teal colored dress and a Pastel colored dress. He looked at both of them, "Teal!" He beamed at me, "Really? Okay!" I said and put it in front of me, while looking at the mirror, it looked quite good.

I slowly felt familiar hands on my waist, he was staring at me, "What are you looking at Abraham?" I asked him as he rested his chin on my shoulder, "How can someone look so pretty all the time?" He replied, "Really? How can someone be so cheesy all the time?" I taunted him, he frowned cutely and "I have to change." I said and pecked his lips and before he could react I ran back to the changing room. I undressed and hopped into the dress, it looked as good as it looked in the mirror.

I went out and searched for Abraham who was looking at a gown, "Abraham!" I called him, he shifted his gaze towards me and eyed me from top to bottom, "You look great." He flashed his million dollar smile, a smile alone that could end all wars. "Thank you!" I said.

I looked behind him, at the gown he was holding, noticing me seeing the gown he spoke, "Oh! Scar, please wear this." He said excitedly, "But Abraham I have bought the wedding dress." I told him, "Hmph! I know! But I loved this in a look, please, for me." He pleaded with puppy dog eyes knowing I cannot resist them. "Okay." I smiled and took the Peach colored, sleeveless gown.

I went into the changing room and took off the dress, I hopped into the gown which was exactly my size and looked absolutely beautiful. Nervously, I went out to Abraham who had his back towards me, before I could speak Mark exclaimed with a burger in his hands, "Scarlette! Oh my God! You look out of world!" Abraham turned back, he eyed me from top to bottom with wide eyes and mouth hanging. I guess he did not realize but he was staring at me as if trying to absorb something. "Speak!" I hissed, "You...heaven...fabulous! You look fantastic and...Perfect!" he said and I could feel blood rushing in my cheeks and making them go red. "Thank you!" I said as he just kept looking at me.

Suddenly his face fell, "But you have got your wedding dress." He sighed sadly, "Are you out of your mind?" I said, he looked up and raised his eyebrows. "I'm getting this for the wedding. That dress...I will wear on the bridal shower. But this one is surely fixed to be worn on the wedding!" I told him, his face lit up like 1000 volt bulb. "Thank You. It is really very pretty!" I told him, "My choices are always pretty." He winked at me and went away.

He is such a cutie, my cute little cheese ball!

I went inside the changing room again, changed into my Denim jeans and White T-shirt that said, "Awesome kids don't dance." in a weird font, though I dance and I am awesome but Abraham loves this t-shirt and carried both the dresses in my shopping bag. I took both of them and went to the cashier. She was a fair girl in black leather pants, white button up shirt and hair up in a bun. She was wearing glasses with minimal makeup but bright red lips.

"Anything else madam?" She said sweetly in a shrill voice, "No that is it. Thank you so much!" I replied, she smiled. "10,000 madam." She said handing me the bill. Before I could take out my wallet I saw Abraham handing his card to the girl, I held his hand, "Abraham! What are you doing?" I asked him. "Paying for my girlfriend's dresses." He replied as if it was a casual thing. "No you are not. You already have your expenses; do not spend your money on me." I scolded him, "Okay! I will only pay for the gown, which I chose for you, okay! That is my Valentine's day gift." He said and took my card from my hand, "5000 from each of the cards lady." He said nicely to the girl.

"Here sir," she handed him our cards, "Want to take our survey mister?" She asked Abraham and I noticed her tone changed from sweet to sexy, he looked at me, I shrugged, "Okay!" He said shrugging casually. "Your name?" She asked, "Abraham Khan." He replied, I could see she was not writing anything.

She then did the cheapest thing in the world, she opened top button of her shirt, "It is hot." She said winking at Abraham as I rolled my eyes and he made a confused face. I was burning inside, she knew I was his girlfriend and she was doing all this right in front of me, "Your phone number?" She continued. Now this was absolutely ridiculous!

I interrupted, "Uh, Lady! We are not here to play 20 questions, I guess. Can you please hand us the bill?" I said sternly and rudely, she scowled at me and held the bill towards Abraham, of course to hold his hand, I snatched the bill from her and stormed off.

"Woah! Woah! Woah! Babe, what is wrong?" Abraham held me and asked, "Didn't you see that she was just flirting with you, not taking some stupid survey? She was taking advantage of your sweetness, and, you too were answering her questions like a fool! That bloody bitch!" I flared in anger.

"I didn't see that but I see you are kind of jealous, aren't you?" He asked, *Yes because I love you*, my brain said, "Oh please! I do not even care a single bit." I said and went out of the store. He pulled me back and pressed his lips to mine, relaxing me under his magic and touch. "I love you and only you. None of these open buttoned bitches can attract me, because I am already yours! Truly, madly, deeply, completely yours. Okay?" He calmed me down. "Yes." I whispered happily.

Soon the others came out, "Why did you fly out of the store like this?" Jessica asked me, "She got jealous!" Isabella and Mark cooed and I rolled my eyes at them, "The lady at the counter was flirting with him and he could not realize that so I got a bit irritated." I explained her, "That is called being jealous!" Mark spoke and I ignored him again.

"I am not going to cook now, very tired!" Ell stretched her arms, "Let us go to Nandos! I love it!" Mark jumped and we nodded in acceptance.

We had a happy lunch together and went to our respective houses.

Chapter 21

<u>Abraham</u>

Scarlette has been crazily happy since the last few days; she has been giggling and laughing on the most stupid things in the world. I guess it was because day after tomorrow is Ashley and James' wedding or maybe something else. I saw the time on my laptop which was two in the morning. I shut my laptop and laid down next to her, I put my arms around her waist and pulled her close to my chest, she looked so peaceful and calmed down while sleeping, I go bananas barely by looking at the slight smile on her face when she sleeps.

I removed her hair from her face, stroked her forehead and kissed it, "Good night Barbie doll." I kissed her cheek and saw her smile, "Good night Abraham." She replied in a sleepy and sexy voice before I felt her snoring again.

I have always notice the little things about her, like the way she talks, the way her eyes light up every time she sees me. And when she scolds me, instead of getting angry I fall in love with her harder. She is everything I always wanted, without her here, life is just a lie. I have found my one true love in Scarlette. Her eyes, her smile, her laugh, her cuteness, everything causes joy in me that cannot be described. She reminds me of diamonds, and of stars twinkling in the night sky. She is like everything good in the world rolled into one. And I love her. I love her more than I could possibly feel. I know she is special. I think she is something rather great. She is my anchor, the only thing keeping me from floating away.

And I cannot wait until she wakes up so that I can tell her that I love her. I cannot wait until she wakes up because I want her to open her eyes and see a glimmer of hope that makes her reality much better than her dreams. When she wakes up I want her to see something that is the beginning to a whole new life, something greater than it was I cannot wait until she wakes up so that the first thing she can see is me. I cannot wait until she wakes up so that I tell her that I want to marry her and declare to the world that she is mine and I am her Valentine forever, that she is my life and I want her to be with me till death do us apart.

But I am waiting for something else also, the red light. The time when all of this would come to an end. Because it was simply far too good to be true, and I had been living this dream for far too long. When would it end? When would the time come where everything would come crashing down? It had to come soon. Nobody got to live the life they wanted. Not if you are someone like me anyway- a person who has killed someone.

Thinking of the consequences I drifted off to sleep with the best thing in the world cuddled in my arms, Scarlette, my Scarlette.

Next morning, I woke up to the piercing rays of the sun, I hate to wake up early in the morning and put my hand on the other side to wake Scarlette up but to my surprise she was not there. I got up slowly and walked out of our room and down to the kitchen, she was nowhere in the house. Suddenly, something caught my eye, there was a piece of paper stuck on the refrigerator with a magnet, it said-

'*Hey Abraham,*

Good morning. I had to buy some grocery, there is nothing in the house to eat except milk; we do not include that in the above line because technically we <u>drink</u> milk. Lol xD I know it is funny, anyway, I thought to wake you up but you looked too cute in your sleep. Do not go back to sleep after this, freshen up and let me remind you that today is Ashley's bridal shower. The boys and girls will be here by three.

Love you,

Scarlette xx'

Sighing sadly as I saw the clock strike noon I dragged myself to the washroom, I freshened up and lightened my stubble. I hopped in for a nice and long shower and after a good thirty minutes came out of the bathroom. Not wanting to dress up a lot I wore a comfortable grey t-shirt, navy blue hoodie and black jeans.

A little while later, I heard the door open and practically ran downstairs, "Morning babe!" I wished as I hugged, "It is already 1:30 in the evening, why are you wishing me morning?" She spoke in a thick voice and I pulled away to see her face. She was not excited or happy anymore, she had her eyes and nose swollen and red. She had been crying?

"Hey babe, what is wrong? Why are you crying?" I cupped her face but she shook her head, "I am not crying, it is cold outside and I got a bit of cough and cold." She shrugged

She turned to me, "Hungry?" I nodded; she kept all the things and keys on the couch. She never does that, all things are kept properly if they belong to Scarlette John Waters.

She turned around and started making lunch and coffee. "What is wrong?" I asked her, she shook her head in denial, "Are you sure?" I asked her and she nodded with a small smile. "Can you please set the plates?" She asked me in a low voice and I nodded, "Sure."

"Why are you so sad?" I asked her she sighed in annoyance, "Because my sister is getting married today! Can't I be emotional and nostalgic?" She yelled but took a deep breath, "Sorry."

She was cutting vegetables without any singing or smile on her face unlike what she usually does. "What's my baby doing?" I said and snaked my arms on her waist, she jumped a little in shock. "Abraham what are you doing? You scared me!" She turned to me with anger, I held her firmly and leaned in. She pushed me back a little, "I cannot always be romancing Abraham! I am cooking." She turned back to making food.

Understanding that she might be having periods or might have had a fight with someone I decided that keeping shut was the safest option. She came and set the bowls on the table, served food for me and handed me the plate before serving herself. We ate in silence, smelling her mood I decided to remain quite.

"I have washed my dishes, after eating go and keep yours I will wash after returning back at night. I am going to get ready." She said and went to the room, without any smile on her face.

As soon as I finished doing the dishes, Scarlette had to do them at night but she was upset, I did not want her to come back and clean the dishes after a tiring day. The bell rang pulling me out of my thoughts; I went and opened the door as I heard her showering, "Hey man!" Everyone entered one by one.

"Where is Scarlette?" Jessica, in a black t-shirt and blue denims, asked me. "She is showering." I replied and all of them nodded. Soon I heard footsteps descending the staircase and I turned around to see Scarlette come down in an oversized flower printed maxi dress. "You look good!" Jennifer, who was wearing a plain black jumpsuit, said with a big grin but in reply received a small smile.

"Okay," Jessica turned the attention towards her, "So the bridal shower starts at 6. So, basically, you guys and we have get ready by 5" Jessica told us. "Venue?" Oliver asked her, she took out the card from her pocket, "Uhm, it is Wedding Paradise Club" we nodded.

"Girls, we have only 2 hours to get ready so le-" Shawn interrupted her, "2 hours is not *only*!" He gasped, "You have to get manicure, pedicure, hair spa, make up, threading and changing done?" Jennifer asked, "Oh, um, okay. They are only." Shawn nodded.

"Good, so let's go to the salon first and then we'll come back home and change." she said as they nodded, "And us?" We asked them with puckered lips. "You guys also take a nap, a bath; make your hair and change. We'll be back by then!" Isabella smiled at us as we nodded helplessly.

Ellie

At 4

We returned from the salon after getting threading, waxing, manicure and pedicure done. "We are back loves!" Jessica yelled as we entered the house. "We missed you!" Oliver whined as they came to the living room but...without Abraham and Jacob. "Where are Abraham and Jacob?" I asked them, Oliver looked at me, he appeared frozen.

"Are the girls home yet?" Jacob yelled behind us entering, while looking at his phone and showing something to Abraham who was smiling madly. He looked up as Scarlette and I raised eyebrows, their smiles changed into fear.

Abraham

"Jacob and Abraham? From where huh?" Ell asked us, "We... we went to...get ice cream" I managed to lie. "Ice cream?" Scarlette said in a voice laced with confusion. "Want? Vanilla?" I asked her, she shook her head side to side, "Nah thanks" I raised my eyebrows to the others who shook their heads instead of Mark, obviously.

"These boys," Jessica shook her head and turned attention towards her, I smiled at her; she smiled back a bit before pulling off her normal face again, "Come, and let us get ready." She said to the girls, "Boys go get ready we should not get late!" She ordered us before leaving with the girls.

After they went off, "Phew! That was close" Jacob sighed heavily, "Yeah! Thank me I wanted to have ice cream otherwise Ell would have turned her question paper mode on!" I said, "True." He chuckled. "Where did you guys go?" Shawn asked us, "Oliver and Jessica know!" I smiled at Oliver.

"Thank her! She saved you both" he laughed lightly as we nodded. "Can we know?" Mark asked impatiently referring 'we' as Shawn and Mark. "We are proposing our girlfriends for marriage tomorrow." I whispered to them so that none of the girls heard us talking, "YOU ARE WHAT!?" Mark yelled after which I slapped him.

"What's up Mark?" Isabella appeared from the staircase, "He is mad, Abraham said that he is gay and loves him so he got scared." Oliver laughed and she gave a disgusted and confused expression before eyeing me, "Oh, okay!" She said and walked back upstairs as I glared at Oliver who shrugged sheepishly.

"Mate, none of the girls know about this except Jessica. So shh!!" I told him while putting finger on my lips, "Sorry." he whispered. "We went to get a ring for Ell because I did not buy while he already did." Jacob said in a low voice, "Calls for a party!" Shawn whispered and all the boys hugged us in congratulations.

Jacob thought I had bought a ring but in reality I was proposing Scarlette with the same ring that Alisha had given me for proposing Sarah.

My phone pinged, MESSAGE FROM SISTER IN LAW, it said. "I like the name you saved!" Oliver said and patted my back. I smiled at him as I opened her message-

"Abraham and Jacob, you guys suck at lying. You're welcome xD anyway, I'm happy. Send me the pictures of the rings. Proud of you brother in law ;)"

"Brother in law?" Oliver asked me, "Check what she has my number saved in her phone as." he smiled goofily, he laughed shaking his head, "Reply and go change or they will kill us" he said and went off.

I replied, "No Jessica, I cannot. You see the ring in Scarlette's finger tomorrow. Please, you know I love you sister in law xx" I sent her. "Huh, too much. Okay! But propose her tomorrow. Now go and change. Yes right, I love you too brother-in-law xx" I went off to my room.

I entered my room to see Scarlette standing in her teal colored dress, in front of the mirror. "You look stunning" I said to her, "Huh?" she turned to me, "Oh, Abraham. Thanks" she said timidly and nervously. She looked unsure, she was wearing her teal colored dress, hair in a fancy bun with curled flicks on the sides, she was yet to do her makeup but she looked perfect to me.

"And why are you nervous?" I asked as I saw that nervousness in her eyes, "I don't know, I'm not confident that I look suitable for a bridal party. It's...over the top" She confessed before gulping, "Oh come on babe! You look out of the world. It's perfect; saw Isabella's excitement level and her magenta gown? Looks like it's her bridal shower!" I stated. "You...sure?" She asked me, "Yes my love" I kissed her cheek.

"Now go and change" She told me, I nodded and went to the closet to get his tuxedo. As I came out she was wearing black kohl, mascara and a thin stroke of eye liner with a bright red lipstick and a tad bit of blush. I eyed her from top to bottom as she did the same, "You" both of said at the same time and laughed.

I pointed towards her to go first, "You look fabulous!" She said to me and I bit my lip blushing, "Thank you." I said, "That red lipstick makes you look even hotter" I said and chuckled, it was her turn to blush now, "Thank you." she smiled and said.

"Love birds!!!" Shawn cried from downstairs, "Make out later!!" He yelled, we laughed and went down. "Why the fuck are you always shouting Shawn?" Jennifer said as she descended the stairs along with the girls, he turned back with a straight face but as he laid his eyes on them he raised his eyebrows.

He whistled, "Look there come the goddesses from heaven!" he smirked. "Let us go!" Jessica said coming in the room, I eyed her; she looked beautiful in her yellow dress.

"You look beautiful." I heard Scarlette whisper into the phone to Ashley, she giggled and whispered back "You too sister! I will miss you so much," She wiped her tears away before disconnecting the call.

After we reached the door, Ashley in between and all of us with our girlfriends. We were supposed to enter parallel to one another, we walked in. All the gazes were on us like we were some kind of aliens; I smiled at Scarlette's ENTIRE family.

As soon as we entered, we suddenly realized why Scarlette always said that her family was nothing less than a full country. She linked her arms with mine, she smiled and blinked once, this was our little way of saying "chill" but now she meant with "They won't eat you. They are good people"

"Oh heaven! Scarlette, after so long!" A lady in her mid-forties wearing a black dress and a super strong perfume, I was almost going to sneeze, hugged Scarlette, "Hello Olivia aunt!" she said, freeing herself from the embrace. "Hello young man!" She greeted me warmly, "Hello aunt!" I replied to which she frowned and I gave Scarlette a tough time struggling to stifle her giggle. "Call me Olivia Rose!" she smiled, I smiled back, "Let us meet the others! We have been so eager to see you both" she said and led us to the other members.

There were around 10 people I met after which I met Scarlette's grandmother, "Hello grand mum." Ashley hugged an old lady on wheel chair. "Hello Scarlette my baby! How are you? I missed you much! No one can replace my babies you know." she said tenderly and looked up at me, "So, you are Abraham Khan? The boy our daughter has given her heart to?" She inquired; I nodded and smiled at her, "Hello madam! I am Abraham Khan, singer of Groove" I gave my hand. "Hello son! I am Annabelle Jenner. Ashley's mother's mother." she introduced herself, "Reason why she is so spoilt!" Scarlette laughed as she told.

"Oh dear! We were so eager to meet you and," she looked at me, "your fiancée." I choked on my breath and Scarlette inhaled a sharp breath. "Grand mum! He is not, uh, um, my f-fiancée." she stammered as she corrected her and grand mum widened her eyes in shock, I nodded even though I knew tomorrow she will be my fiancée.

"You have not proposed her yet?" She asked me, I bit my lip and looked at Scarlette with helpful eyes, "Grandma! Please one should be ready also!" She said saving me. "Who is not?" Her grandma asked shocked, "Both of us." she closed her eyes annoyance.

Later we were called by someone, "Scarlette and Abraham it is time for the cake cutting." we went off to the cake table, forgetting her grandma's confusion and enjoying the night.

Enjoying I guess was only for me and the others because Scarlette appeared lost and depressed ever since she came back from the grocery shopping. She has never been so quiet and in deep thought until and unless she is reading a book but right now she was not smiling at all.

Chapter 22

<u>Scarlette</u>

I woke up early in the morning to the sound of chirping birds and piercing sunlight. I changed into my peach wedding gown Abraham had bought me. Ashley had assigned each of us a stylist so that we looked "out of the world for" her "freaking wedding!" As she said. My and Ellie's stylist was one of our very close friends May Cordan.

I changed and went straight to her, "Oh my! Someone is looking perfect!" She complimented, "Thank you May." I smiled at her, "Abraham is never going to tear his gaze away." she teased me, I swat her arm playfully. "Oh yes, I will not." Abraham said as he entered the room in a handsome black tuxedo.

"Oh! Look!" She stared at something behind me; I turned around to see Ellie and Jacob coming down hand in hand with smiles as if they had just become the President of the United States of America. "Spit it out! Fast!" May crossed my arms in curiosity. Instead of replying Ellie squealed and ran in my direction, she stopped in front of me, "I am engaged!!!" She squealed. It took me some minutes to process what she said, engaged and Ellie? Wait! Jacob? What?

"Jacob? You proposed her? Wait! You guys are getting... married?" I asked them shockingly, they nodded with extra-large grins. "Yes...it is official. We are going to get married." Jacob said and both of them blushed together. "Congratulations Jacob and Ellie!" I hugged each of them with a smile.

"Oh heaven! Congratulations you two! Jacob you bitch you would have told me at least told me...once" May hugged them together, "Ellie is going to say the same thing to Abraham very soon!" he grinned at me mischievously and I raised my eyebrows.

"What does he mean?" I asked Abraham innocently. I looked at Jacob who had a grin plastered on his face, I turned back to him, "I do not know." He replied back and I furrowed my eyebrows and stared at him but eventually shrugged it off.

"Show me the ring." I said curiously, Ellie put up her right hand and I admired it with stars in my eyes. I so badly wanted to flip places with Ellie and Jacob but I could not. She showed me her ring, how much I wanted Abraham to put a ring in my finger too but I could not say yes to him even if he did. God is so cruel at times. I was happy for her but there was something deep inside me that was jealous of her badly. I sighed lightly while I admired the beautiful platinum love band.

The boys went away to get James while we hid a beautiful Ashley who was wearing a gorgeous white gown, behind the curtain. I was a bit lost, my best friend cum sisters were going to get married, Ellie and Ashley. "Scarlette?" Ellie called me; I plastered a smile on my face and turned back, "All happens for good. Now cheer up!" She smiled and hugged me. I was not at all on agreeing by her words, what was going to happen was not going to happen for good, it was going to throw both of us apart however hard I tried.

"Let us go. It is already 9:30am." Ashley called us and we sat down in the carriage for the bride and the bridesmaids. We entered the church after a 10 minute journey, we saw James, in a handsome tuxedo waiting for his bride to be, Ashley. His face immediately lit up like a thousand stars at the sight of his bride, in a lavish white gown and purple orchids.

The ceremony begun, we stood next to our boyfriends/fiancés. Abraham linked his arms with mine; I held the banquet in one hand and his hand in the other.

"Ashley, do you consent to be my wife?" James asked her, finding their worlds into each other's eyes. "I do." She nodded happily.

"James, do you consent to be my husband?" She asked him, "I do." He nodded.

They together took the vows, "We take each other as husband and wife and promise to love each other truly for better, for worse, for richer, for poorer, in sickness and in health, till death us do part." I could see Ashley's eyes watering already. Only I knew how bad I was feeling, not because I was seeing my sister getting married but because I hated to be like this, to do what I was about to do but did not want to.

"What God joins together man must not separate. May the Lord confirm the consent that you have given, and enrich you with his blessings." The priest blessed them, "Now you may kiss the bride" he said. They shared a long kiss as if they complete one another.

At Afternoon

Abraham

I requested Ashley to ask all to wear the same dresses or tuxedos they wore to the wedding to the party. "Why?" She asked me, I covered her mouth as she tried to push me. "I am proposing Scarlette...for marriage" I quickly whispered. I knew she would shout so I had covered her mouth.

I stared at me, "Do not shout!" I warned her and removed my hand. "You are proposing Scarlette? Really?" She asked me in shock, "No I am kidding!" I said sarcastically and she rolled her eyes before pulling me into a hug, "You have made me happier!" she smiled at me. "Do not spill it out and just ask all to wear the same dresses okay?" I warned and asked her, she nodded readily, "I am with you in the mission Abraham Khan!" She said and went off.

I rolled my eyes and went to Scarlette.

I set my hair and stuffed my phone into my pocket. I opened my drawer and took out a red pouch, it had the ring. The ring that was going to be in Scarlette's finger in a little time. I stuffed it into my pocket and went out to find my girl, smiling at me.

Scarlette

I saw Abraham coming out of our room with a handsome smirk and perfect hair in the same black tuxedo. "Hi" I said to him, "Hi there" he chuckled. Again, he held my hand and went out to the others. Every time he showered me with his love, a bit of me dead because I was lying to him.

We entered a beautiful lawn, decorated with white lights, blue and purple orchids with a bridge to the left under which was flowing a water body. It looked prettier than anything in the world.

After the family formalities, dance (which we sucked at) and a little drinks only our close family was left and my friends. Abraham called me, "Bored?" He asked me, I nodded and whispered "Very". "A walk?" He asked me, "Great!" I said and he intertwined his fingers with mine.

The bridge was suspiciously empty, "Why is it empty?" I asked him.

"Let's not let it be" He said and we walked to the bridge.

Ellie

Abraham and Scarlette walked towards the bridge; it looked beautiful and was obviously very firm. They walked over the calm water that flowed under the bridge, surrounded by the calm and quite surroundings as all the relatives whispered to themselves.

"I love the way our fingers look intertwined," Abraham said as his eyes sparkled like the only star in the sky. It was dark then but all of us could still see his glowing face and perfect quiff. "But you know what would make them look even prettier?" He asked her, "What?" she asked back.

"If we both were wearing rings," he stopped walking and looked up; his smiling eyes met her confusingly shocked ones.

He held my hand just before he knelt down, he looked at me with the biggest grin as little tears of pure happiness and joy welled up in her eyes.

"I cannot imagine growing old with anyone else, nor do I want to. I know you're the only one I want to share my imperfections with for the rest of my life Scarlette Waters. The story of our love is only beginning. Let us write our own happy ending... Will you marry me Scarlette?" His eyes sparkled as they looked up at her.

All of us were on the verge of bursting due to joy and happiness; all the three sisters had found their husbands on the same day. Ashley had got married while Scarlette and I were about to get married. I was waiting for her to say yes and to go and hug her.

"I do not love you anymore Abraham." She turned to walk away as tears blurred her vision and everyone stared at them with shock and confusion, Abraham kept sitting on his knees even after she walked away as if trying to absorb her answer. The ring fell down from his hands and all of a sudden the clouds rushed to his defense and did not let anyone see that tears of betrayal and sadness that were flowing from his eyes.

All of us rushed inside to save our costly dresses.

Chapter 23

<u>Abraham</u>

I still could not believe my ears. Scarlette said she did not love me anymore and I was thinking of being with her forever. The red light was here, it had come at the least expected time. I ran quickly to our room in the guest house where we were staying since morning, "What the fuck Scarlette?" I yelled as I barged into our room.

She wiped her crocodile tears away, "I am sorry Abraham, I-I cannot do this anymore." She said looking at the floor and something in me said that she was lying. "Stop lying Scarlette, I know you love me. What is bothering you?" I asked her, she shook her head before sobbing, "It is nothing Abraham and I do not feel anything for you anymore." She shook her head in denial.

"Please Scarlette, say that you are lying, say that you want to marry me and say that you love me. Please, if you want we will not marry right now but please do not dump me like this." I literally begged in front of her but she did not say anything.

"You used me for helping you for your surgery! I have understood how selfish you are! You could have asked me to just lend you money but you did not because you wanted to hurt me!" I yelled and she kept looking at the floor without a word.

Instead of saying anything she leaned in and kissed me, it felt like our final one. It was different, it was mixed with my tears as our lips molded perfectly with each other. She pulled away and gave a sigh that sounded like a final sigh, like the final breath of someone who might die any moment.

And although she showed no emotion, her eyes were more broken than I had ever seen. With one last look and one last small and whimsy smile, she nodded and went away, "Bye, Abraham." Then she was out of the door, heading outside into the cold night air. And I did not stop her, because I could not.

I dragged my broken self to the backyard that was now wet because the rain had stopped. Picking up three bottles of whisky, I chugged them down one after the other and started punching the wall next to me, I was high but nothing mattered to me more than my broken heart and that feeling of getting betrayed in me.

"Hey Abraham stop!" Isabella ran to me and held my hand, "What are you d-" as I turned to her she stopped, "Are you high?" She inquired, "No officer, I am Abraham." I burst into a fit of giggles and she just rolled her eyes.

"Have it." Isabella handed me the sandwich she was eating which I gladly accepted. I tried to eat with my right hand but the fingers were frozen so I ate with my left. She kept looking at me as I was finishing the huge and delicious cheese sandwich.

"What did you do?" She said checking my hand.

"Ate the sandwich." I replied.

"Did you break your knuckles?" She tried to move my fingers but they did not, "Yes you did." She answered her question on her own.

"You should not do all this. It is bad for you."

I guffaw, wiping my mouth with the sleeve of my tuxedo, "You know what is funny?" I said, still chewing. "How everyone keeps telling me that. That is so funny!"

"Maybe you should listen to them."

I shook my head a hundred times, "No, because, the last time I listened to someone, she broke my heart into a million pieces and left me to rot. And you know something?" I took another mouthful. "Maybe it is not everyone else, maybe it is just me. Maybe I am the bad guy. And no matter who I surround myself with, it is always going to me who fucks it all up."

"Abraham, please do not say that." Isabella held my hand.

"I am lot of things, Isabella." I nod, chewing in thought, "I am a lot of things but I am not a liar I was one before but not anymore and she is a liar! She was a liar before and she still is a liar!" I yelled at the sky.

I put the half eaten sandwich on the plate, looking down at the bread as if it is going to tell me why she hurt me. I suddenly feel pain within me, pain that I do not want to feel. *Her.* I felt as if I had swollen a huge glass article.

I shake my head again, trying to shake out *her.* And I started hitting myself, and I started punching myself. Because I had get *her* out of my thoughts and feelings. I wanted to forget all of it that had ever happened between us, I wanted to forget *her* because she felt nothing for me.

"Abraham? Abraham!" Isabella tried to grab my bleeding hands. I just kept shaking my head, trying to pull myself out of her grasp.

"Abraham you need to fucking calm down!" she cried.

I pulled myself out of her grasp and put my head in my hands, pressing the heels of my palms against my closed eyes. My knuckles were paining and bleeding but it was not bigger than the pain in my heart. "I cannot do it, Isabella." I felt warm water well in my eyes.

"I know that. Abraham, I *know* that. However, if she is lying can you imagine how she must be feeling right now?"

I could and I did not. Because the mental image I had was more than enough to push someone over the edge. I was so close already; I did not want to fall. "Just stop it."

"Abraham-"

"STOP IT!"

She silenced and I just started shaking.

"No, no, no." I hit myself again, "No! Stop it! Shut up! Just shut the fuck up!" I yelled and I bet she was scared of me acting the way I was, but I could not control myself to turn it all off.

"I do not give a living shit." I said simply, following the ant running along the pavement. "I do not give a shit about any of it."

"I know you do," she said, "You have always taken care of Scarlette, at least ever since I have seen. You always have!"

"No, no, no." I shook my head again, "No. I cannot!"

"It does not have to be this way-"

"It does!" I yelled, making her jump. "Of course it does! I suffocated both of them, I killed them. Just that Sarah gave up but Scarlette did not and instead chose to leave me and face the shit of life all alone! I am the worst person-"

"Abraham, you are not-"

"You spoke again? Shut up! Just shut the fuck up! There are two types of people in the world, Isabella. One who step on the little ants and the others who make way for them. I am the ant crusher, I am the ant crusher, I go out of my way on purpose to step on all of them and kill them. Because I simply do not care,

I have never and I never will. This is what happens... people get close to me and then they get hurt and then they leave me."

"You know that is not the truth."

"It was never meant to be!" I laughed at myself, holding my arms out wide. "It was never going to happen, Isabella! *Fuck*, I am a fool. I got fucking fooled! How could I possibly think all this would *actually* work out? Fucking shit!"

She just looked at me, unsure as to what to say.

"Good things like Scarlette do not happen to people like me, Isabella." I smiled, although it did not reach till the corner of my eyes like I had felt it doing many times before. "People like me, we just get trails. They make you *think* like you have got it all, and just when you are enjoying it, it all gets swept out from under your feet. It is the universe's way of showing what you can have, whilst making it damn sure you know damn well what you cannot have."

I stood up and spread my arms out wide, looking up at the sky. "I hear you universe!" I screamed. "I have got the message, loud and clear! Good one! You sure pulled one over on me! Next time, can you not make the trail so believable! Fuck you, universe!"

"Abraham, come on." Isabella stood up and tried to wrap her arms around my body, but I pushed myself away from her and moved further into darkness.

"Are you happy?" I screamed, pointing up at the sky. "Are you up there grinning now? Now that you have got what you always wanted? I am officially fucked up and ruined! Well done! Mission Accomplished!" I clapped.

And then I collapsed on the wet and cold grass, and although I did not cry, I felt much worse. The pain was there, I just could not cry it out. I banged my fists against the ground until they were frozen and covered the dirt. I rocked myself back and forth. I was numb. Everything had become numb.

"Abraham you are fucking scaring me." Isabella rushed to my side, trying to pull me up, "Abraham, come inside. Please. I will make you some tea. Abraham!"

However, I did not bulge, and eventually she stopped trying. I guess she too was crying too much to see what she was doing and she was getting too cold. Because then she left, and I was left all alone. Just like I was always supposed to be.

I was still rocking back and forth when I heard the door flung open and heavy footsteps coming my way. I did not look because I did not have the guts to do so.

"Abraham, come on inside now. It is cold out." Jacob's voice is tough, but there is a hint of empathy. He tugged at my sides and I just kept shaking.

"I want to die," I tell him.

And then he picked me up in his arms and carried me inside. And then I slipped into cold, harsh and lonely darkness.

I woke up with a hammering head and stinging eyes at my own bedroom. I turned around to see the empty room, there was no one around. I looked towards the bedside table to see a note, it said-

"Hi Abraham,

How are you? Actually, you fainted last night after your massive emotional breakdown and I had to call Jacob to take you home. Next to the note are some pain killers and a glass of water for the hangover of three bottles of beer. Please take rest today and do not worry.

Loves,

Isabella Nelson xx."

As I was about to pick up the medicine and the glass my hand ached and I saw my knuckles plastered. I tried to move my hand but was unable to do so, my right hand was broken and it absolutely sucked.

I gulped the sour tablet and drank the water. "Scarlette!" I called her but got no reply, "Scarlette!" I called again still receiving no reply from her. I walked down the stairs before having a tough time dragging myself out of the bed. I searched around the entire house but did not find her anywhere.

I tried calling on her number but it was not reachable. I called up Ashley, "Hey Ashley. Is Scarlette there?" I asked her hurriedly, "Uhm no, I do not think so. She left right after you both…uh right whatever." She hesitated and I nodded, "Thank you." I said and disconnected the call.

I called up everyone from my mother to her mother but none of them had any idea where Scarlette was. Suddenly something caught my eyes, it was a box wrapped in red gift wrapping paper. I tore it carelessly to reveal a dairy that said- "I know you hate me for doing this, but I had to do this." Scribbled in Scarlette's handwriting.

I opened the dairy to see that every page had our picture on the either side with cute captions written neatly. Some were candid shots in which we were not posing but were either looking at each other or one of us was looking at the other. The second last page had a picture of me looking at her where she had no idea I was seeing her, placed above a picture of her looking at me where I had no idea she was seeing me from Ashley and James' wedding.

I turned over the last page that read- "*I am so sorry for doing this to you but I am doing it for your good. I never had any intention to use you or your money; I am leaving you for our good. You deserve someone way better Abraham. Please forgive me and try to forget me. I am going away and I will never come back. No, I am not dying, I am living for the sake of your good and I hope you never know what I mean. Always remember, I still love you Abraham. Remember, nobody's feelings are more important than your own so take time to love yourself too. And you can love someone so much but cannot always be with them. Scarlette xx.*"

Tears found their way out of my eyes and nothing but pain and misery took over me. She left me absolutely alone without an explanation with her last words that she still loves me. What kind of a love was this that I always got? Why did my other half always left me alone without an explanation? Why I was the one to be hurt the most? Who does she think she is?

My eyes soon felt heavy, but so did my heart. And it absolutely sucked. Sucked was clearly an understatement.

"But you promised me Scarlette Waters!" I yelled at the top of my lungs, "You fucking broke your promise! You promised to be with me till infinity, this is your infinity? I fucking hate you Scarlette! I hate you!" I said throwing a photo of ours on the floor.

I thought I had somebody to care but she was just there to break me and shatter me into millions of pieces.

And then I met with silence, it was creeping in just like it always does. I tried to outrun it but it only followed me closely. And I do not move, instead I just sat on the floor, looking at the walls with a solemn expression. It felt as if the walls were getting closer by each passing second just to eat me up. Why did love have to hurt so much?

I felt rather sick at that point of time, but nothing could get rid of the poison inside of me.

Chapter 24

5 years later

"Saira! Oh my God where were you? I have been finding you ever since forever!" My boss came rushing behind to me as we made the last minute preparations of a two day charity event called 'Believe in Magic' that was being hosted by our event organizing company called 'Lights and Stars event organizer'. I know it is weird.

"Yes Mrs. Braganza," I turned to my boss running behind me in a white shirt, yellow skirt with yellow coat tucked in. She flipped her bobby cut hair behind her ears. "Dear it would be really sweet if you please do me a small and cute little favor?" She said sugar coating her words as always.

Mrs. Julia Braganza was the CEO of our company and was the youngest looking 50 year old lady. She runs around and gets excited just like teenagers do, she is a lady of bright colors that never included colors like brown or grey. She was one of the most stylish oldies I had ever seen in my life.

I nodded her to go on, "The main host, Noel Johnson, has met with a car accident and is very critical," She spoke, "Oh my God! I hope she does well!" I gasped, "Oh we wish the same sweetheart! We want a beautiful girl who is confident and has a nice voice." She spoke.

"Okay?" I said unsurely, "I want you to go and host the event." She said with requesting eyes, "What? Mrs. Braganza you know I am the head event organizer not the host!" I almost jumped in my place. "Please dear, the event is starting in fifteen minutes and we cannot bring another speaker. We are the top company in Los Angeles and we cannot let our name go down by putting a bad host Saira please!" She said with a puppy dog face that I am unable to reject.

"But I do not know what I have to speak!" I cried and she shook her head, "You just have to read and speak." She smiled and I sighed, "Okay ma'am, I will become the host." Soon I was engulfed in a tight hug by her. "Now go and change as quickly as you can because you have to greet the chief guest too. He will be here any minute." She said and walked away.

I rolled my eyes and turned away to the changing room, "Hey, I am the new host. Can you please hand me my dress?" I said as I crept in, "Hello, please come in, I am Taylor Venture, the head stylist." My insides smiled as some old memories flashed in front of me. "Aren't you the head organizer? What was your name?" The blonde in a maroon and white short dress thought.

"Yes, I am the head organizer but Noel met with an accident, I am a replacement. My name is Saira Khan."

"Oh…A very nice and different name." She nodded while handing me a packet, "You are telling me." I chuckled. "So is your husband a Muslim?" She asked me and I looked down as old memories flashed in front of my eyes, "Yes, his name is Abraham." I said before turning on my heels and going to the washroom to change but actually tears had welled up in my eyes.

Even after five years of living on the other side of the world in Los Angeles while leaving everyone behind in London and living under the name of Saira Khan, I am still not over my past; the Scarlette Waters is still alive in somewhere. Saira and Scarlette are two poles apart people, while the brown curly haired Scarlette was chirpy and an extrovert the black and straightened haired Saira is serious and more of an introvert.

Yet one thing between them is same, both love the same guy, Abraham Khan.

I changed into the black floor length dress given to me and curled my hair after a very long time, I put them on one side and did the Smokey eye with bright red lip color, the stylist in me still has not died.

I looked at the final reflection in the mirror and I was quite impressed with the look, I saw my old self in that look and I was grateful to do so. I was missing Abraham more than anything that day, it felt as if he was around me but I prayed him to be in London only.

I do not want him to see me after so many years only to come in terms with the most heartbreaking reality ever.

"Saira, are you ready? The chief guest is here!" I heard Mrs. Braganza knock on the door and I quickly walked out, she eyed me, "You look beautiful and different." She beamed and I was about to thank her when she interrupted me, "Go now! He is already here." She said and I quickly rushed backstage where they handed me the mike.

"Hello ladies and gentlemen," I acknowledged everyone in the crowd, "Good Morning to the Believe In Magic charity event organized by Lights and Stars event organizers private limited. I am your host for today and tomorrow and my name is Saira Khan. I request you all to welcome the chief guest of the evening amongst your claps and cheers, Mr." I froze as I saw the name; my palms started sweating and my head felt dizzy. "Saira, speak." Someone hissed.

I took a deep breath before speaking, "Mr. Abraham Khan."

Now I understood why I was feeling as if he was around me, I walked down the stairs to the opened door. I gulped as I took a banquet of flowers from my best friend Danielle, the only person in Los Angeles who knew about my past. She smiled at me sadly and mouthed, "It is okay." To me and I nodded.

Suddenly my eyes were blinded by camera flashes and I covered my eyes because I already had predicted what happened next. I removed my hand and came face to face with...Abraham. He was waving at the crowd and did not notice me but as soon as he looked down at me to take the banquet he too froze in his place.

He looked deep into my eyes and caused deep holes in my soul. They were the most perfect swirls of brown I had seen in a while. They were shades of brown mixed with golden and honey with chocolate brown flakes over them. They were beautiful. I was absolutely spell bound.

"Welcome to Believe in Magic sir." I spoke as tears threatened to spill from my eyes. He was oozing his usual charm as he stood sexily in a black shirt, black pants and grey jacket with a smirk on his lips as he saw me. His hair was perfectly styled and I had to tear my gaze away from him as I realized I might have been staring at him. I quickly turned around and walked back to the stage.

"It is a pleasure to have you here with us Mr. Abraham Khan, welcome to the Believe in Magic charity event. It would be a great honor for us if you please come upon stage and say a few words." I said while looking at everyone but him but I knew he was staring at me. He gladly got up and came up to the stage.

I handed him the mike and stood awkwardly next to him, "Hello Los Angeles!" He greeted the audience and my heart somehow calmed down as his voice flew from his mouth and struck my ear drums. He gave a long and pre written speech to the crowd whilst I kept standing there, feeling awkward.

"I would also take this moment to introduce you all to my close friend present here," He looked at me and I instantly shook my head in denial, "Scarlette Waters?" He mouthed and I widened my eyes and shook my head again, "Saira *Khan*." He said and only I noticed the emphasis he put on the surname before the audience and staff clapped in amazement. "I feel so *nice* to meet you after so long Saira." He pretended to be happy at my presence but actually his comments were sarcastic and were hitting me like a million needles, suddenly he engulfed me in a tight hug.

The hug was tight and secured, "Scarlette," My old name felt so good to hear, "Say I love you to me!" Abraham whispered in my ears and I literally gasped, "What are you saying Abraham are you out of your mind?" I tried to scold him but he hugged me even tighter.

"Say it or I will tell everyone about you *Scarlette*." He said putting emphasis on my name, "I love you Abraham." Even though he was thinking I did not mean it but I did, I genuinely loved him in the past, in the present and will always love him in the future.

"I wish you meant what you said." He said and pulled away, leaving me on the verge of tears but I controlled myself. "It is great to have you here Mr. Khan." I spoke after reviving from my little emotional breakdown; I read the next function on the list that was performance by him.

"It would be a great pleasure and honor for us Mr. Khan if you please perform something for the kids of the Believe in Magic charitable trust." I smiled as the little girls in the audience went gaga over him. I excused myself and went downstairs into the group of my colleagues standing. "Aye bitch you never told us that Abraham Khan was your friend!" One of them squealed, "Abraham's friend…or ex-girlfriend?" Someone else said wiggling her eyebrows. "It is nothing like that guys Abraham was just my fr-" A familiar tune interrupted me and I guess I knew which song that was. My heart was beating against my chest. It was all I could feel. I was as if everything in my chest was hollow but the harsh beating of my heart was about ready to burst.

"You were the light in my life

I have been searching for you all alone, yeah." He belted out the lyrics and I looked up at the stage just to see him already looking at me, tears started blurring my vision, this was the first song he had sung me to sleep.

"I was lost, you were the guide.

Taking me all the way along, all the way right." He was pointing at me as he sat on the edge of the stage and I closed my eyes but the tears were too much to handle.

"I have never been the one who's going to love someone more, someone less, no. I have never been the one to heal the scars of what you have done." I could see he was trying to control his tears mostly because today was the 21st of November.

"You are my healer, healer

But not the one

I can love and live with forever, ever

Believe me now

I just cannot love you forever

If i let all my walls come down to crumble to the ground and tell you, yeah.

If i light up my past,

Would you still

Stay by me and cry with me ever, cry with me ever? Stay with me forever?

I have never been the one who's gonna love that, no.

I will never be the one to shower my love.

You are my healer, healer but not the one

I can love and live with forever and ever.

Believe me now

I just cannot love you forever, ever.

I say whatever it is, whatever it was

I cannot love you anymore.

I cannot love you for your good, for your happiness, I will let you go.

You, my love, I just cannot let you go but I have to let you go..." I was lip syncing the lyrics and by the time he finished both of us were in a pool of tears.

"Sorry, I am quite attached to this song. It reminds me of many fond memories," He then turned to me, "And someone I love a lot." He was trying to make me feel guilty and was very successful in doing so.

"Give me the words; I will take ahead the event. You go home Scar-Saira, please, he is trying to make you feel guilty. You did the right thing, please." Danielle tried to convince me but I was not the one to give up so easily, "This is my job Danielle and I cannot endanger my job and the future of my family for him." I said and confidently walked up to the stage.

"Now that was something to wait for now wasn't it?" I smiled and the entire audience rose in applause, "Thank you Mr. Khan." This was the last time in the first day when I had acknowledged him or took his name. I tried to avoid his eyes completely while they followed me in whatever and wherever I did, I noticed that his eyes had a different kind of light in them and his lips never left that popular and sexy smile.

Suddenly, I saw him getting up and walking over to Danielle and talking to her but she seemed hardly interested, he asked her something and she said no to it. Next thing was pretty weird because he went to Renee, another colleague, and from his actions it was very clear he was flirting with her, he handed her a piece of paper that she accepted gladly and a deep pit of jealousy exploded in me. He walked back to where he was sitting and started looking at me but I looked away and continued my work.

"Thank you everyone for coming and enjoying the event and for making it a grand success, we will be looking forward to see everyone tomorrow too. Thank you Believe in Magic for giving us the opportunity to host this beautiful event. Thank you Mr. Abraham Khan for granting us with pleasure by being here," The last line was pretty double meaning and it made me kind of uncomfortable, "Thank you to the sponsors and the parents of these beautiful children. Wish you have a good night and hope you come tomorrow also." After three long hours, I said wrapping the first day of the event.

As quickly as I could, I walked to the backstage and returned them the mike, "You were so good!" Taylor and Danielle came over and hugged me, "I was so nervous!" I replied, still in their hug. "Girls, please listen." We heard Mrs. Braganza and straightened up, behind her stood Abraham and I held Danielle's hand tighter.

"The young man here, Mr. Abraham Khan," She said pointing to him, "Ma'am please call me Abraham." He interrupted and she nodded with a smile, "The young man here, Abraham, loved the hard work and dedication of you guys that made the event a success. He was very surprised to know that the host was changed in the last minute because Saira was as good as Noel," She said and pointed at me and I smiled at her. "You did so good *Saira*," He said putting emphasis on my name again, "Your first time is always the best." He said and his words clearly had pun intended, I bent my head down and closed my eyes before I felt Danielle touch my shoulder, "Thank you Abraham." I muttered and he smirked.

"Oh dear you never told us Abraham Khan is your friend?" She asked me as I and Danielle froze on our places, "Uh-" Abraham interrupted me, "We met five years back so maybe she forgot to mention it." He then looked at me dead in the eye, "Maybe she forgot me." A light of sadness was visible in his eyes.

"If any of you want pictures with him please come one by one," She spoke and almost all the girls except me and Danielle ran to him, "You want?" I asked Danielle but she shook her head in denial. I turned to walk away to the changing room without looking back as tears found their way out of my eyes.

Chapter 25

<u>Abraham</u>

Flashback

"Abraham are you ready yet?" my assistant, Josh Robinson, knocked at the door of my changing room. I stood looking at the mirror in a black shirt, black pants and grey jacket. I had to fly to Los Angeles to attend an event of the Believe in Magic charitable trust hosted by Lights and Stars something I do not remember.

I was really not in a mood to go out because today, even after five years, I was missing Scarlette. I had promised myself not to think about her but I was unsuccessful in doing so, she is a part of my heart and the oxygen that I am breathing. How can you forget your heart and the air? Moreover, today was the 21st of November, the day Sarah died.

Scarlette never called me back after that day and I did not see her face after our last kiss, the taste of her lips still lingers on my tongue, I have no idea where she is or what she is or is she even alive or not. I have no idea if she still loves me or if she ever did. She left me without an explanation and a goodbye, the least thing that I deserved.

"Abraham? Are you in there?" Josh's voice pulled me out of my thoughts as I wiped away the tears that had flooded my eyes, "Yeah man, I am ready." I said coming out of the door with a small smile. "We are late already but it is pretty weird that Mrs. Braganza, the CEO, is pretty chilled out that we are late. I am very sure her employees must have also got stuck somewhere!" He said like a typical gossip queen or I must say king and I just chuckled.

"Hello ladies and gentlemen," I heard a slightly familiar voice acknowledge everyone in the crowd, "Good Morning to the Believe In Magic charity event organized by Lights and Stars event organizers private limited. I am your host for today and tomorrow and my name is Saira Khan." Oh wow, the girl and I had the same surname and her voice was very familiar but I did not click it.

"Josh have we heard that voice earlier?" I asked Josh but he shook his head. "I request you all to welcome the chief guest of the evening amongst your claps and cheers, Mr." as I was about to enter she stopped, she did not take my name and I had to keep standing near the door. "Mr. Abraham Khan." she spoke and the way she called me 'Abraham Khan' it was very familiar, as if I had already heard her. The accent and the voice was pulling me in that direction and I suddenly grew eager to see this 'Saira Khan'.

Suddenly my eyes were blinded by camera flashes and as I walked in the girl had covered her eyes due to the flashes. I waved at the cheering crowd, the only people who actually loved me, I noticed that the short girl was standing with flowers in her hands, I looked down to take them from her but what I saw made me freeze.

She was...Scarlette. She stood there, looking at me from eyes filled with tears; she looked beautiful as ever in a black body hugging gown and sexy make up. She looked just as she was five years back; she had hair in big curls and dark make up. Her eyes found mine amidst the camera flashes and I was somehow happy to see her after so long.

However my heart suddenly dropped and all the pain that had temporarily gone had then came flying back, doubled in size. And it was like it was closing down on my lungs, and I was struggling to breath. And I could not think of anything rational in that moment. Everything came smashing back down on me and suddenly I was right back to that night, right back to the moment she left. However, I was no longer feeling empty.

"Welcome to Believe in Magic sir." She spoke as tears threatened to spill from her eyes and I just smirked. As soon as she looked away I had to tear my gaze away from her as I realized I might have been staring at her. She quickly turned on her heels and went over the stage.

"It is a pleasure to have you here with us Mr. Abraham Khan, welcome to the Believe in Magic charity event. It would be a great honor for us if you please come upon stage and say a few words." She said and I realized she was looking at everyone but me as I kept staring at her, as soon as she made the announcement I gladly got up and went to the stage.

She handed me the mike and stood awkwardly next to me, I could see on her face how uncomfortable she was feeling, "Hello Los Angeles!" I greeted the audience to receive loud cheers and whistles after which I gave a long, boring and pre written speech to the crowd while stealing glances at her as she kept standing there, feeling awkward as hell.

Soon my mind came up with a fun idea, "I would also take this moment to introduce you all to my close friend present here," I looked at her with a smirk and she instantly shook her head in denial, "Scarlette Waters?" I mouthed and she widened her eyes and shook her head again, "Saira Khan." I said putting emphasis on the surname she had before the audience and staff clapped in surprise because I guess she did not tell anyone about us. "I feel so nice to meet you after so long Saira." I pretended to be happy by her presence but actually my comments were dipped in sarcasm and sassy taunts.

Taking her by surprise I engulfed her in a hug, it was tight and secured. A feeling of nostalgia and sadness took over me and I wanted to hear something from her.

"Scarlette, say I love you to me!" I whispered in her ears and she literally gasped at my words, "What are you saying Abraham are you out of your mind?" she tried to scold me just like she used to do before but I hugged her even tighter to relax her.

"Say it or I will tell everyone about you Scarlette." I said putting emphasis on her name, she sighed, "I love you Abraham." She said and it made me feel so good and right, my ears and heart had been craving to her these words in her voice.

Suddenly I came face to face with reality, she did not mean it and she said that just so that I did reveal her real identity. "I wish you meant what you said." I said to her and pulled away, leaving tears and guilt in her eyes but she seemed to control herself. "It is great to have you here Mr. Khan." She said after taking a number of deep breaths and pressing the bridge of her nose to control her tears.

"It would be a great pleasure and honor for us Mr. Khan if you please perform something for the kids of the Believe in Magic charitable trust." I smiled as the girls in the audience and staff went gaga over me. She excused herself and went downstairs into a group of girls standing near the stage. "Aye bitch you never told us that Abraham Khan was your friend!" I heard one of them squeal, "Abraham's friend…or ex-girlfriend?" Someone else said to her. "It is nothing like that guys Abraham was just my fr-" A familiar tune started and she turned to face the stage with a shocked face.

"You were the light in my life

I have been searching for you all alone, yeah." I belted out the lyrics looking at her and she looked up, somewhere between reality and her tear filled eyes, I found a sense of home and safety. This song was the first song I had sung her to sleep with and released after she left me, I reached to new heights of popularity and success with this song.

"I was lost, you were the guide.

Taking me all the way along, all the way right." I was purposely pointing at her as I sat down on the edge of the stage and she closed her eyes to stop the tears, this was what she always did and I had understood that.

"I have never been the one who's going to love someone more, someone less, no. I have never been the one to heal the scars of what you have done." She opened her eyes and I was trying so hard to control my tears, memories of Sarah and her were going through my brain.

I sang the entire song and saw her lip syncing the lyrics, by the time I hit the last note both of us were in a pool of tears. Suddenly I realized I was in a public place, "Sorry, I am quite attached to this song. It reminds me of many fond memories," I spoke and turned to her, "And someone I love a lot." I could see guilt and sadness in the tears that filled her eyes.

"Give me the words; I will take ahead the event. You go home Scar-Saira, please, he is trying to make you feel guilty. You did the right thing, please." A girl spoke to her while trying to take the sheet of paper in her hands. She was almost going to call her Scarlette which meant she knew about our past which also meant that she knew the reason why Scarlette had left me.

"This is my job Danielle and I cannot endanger my job and the future of my family for him." She said and I was more confused and angry, she had a family which meant she had married someone else and had children with him. She took a deep breath and walked up the stage.

"Now that was something to wait for now, wasn't it?" she smiled and the entire audience rose in applause, "Thank you

Mr. Khan." That was the last time in the first day when she acknowledged me or took my name. She avoided my eyes through the entire event while they never looked away, even when I tried to look at someone else they eventually flew back to Scarlette.

If I wanted to know her side of the story I had to be close to that girl who called her by her old name. Slowly I got up and walked over to that girl. "Hey lady, what is your name?" I asked her, "Danielle." She replied in an uninterested way, "So Danielle, will you go on a date with me?" I asked her, using my charm.

Instead of getting flattered she kept looking ahead, "I know you want to know why she left everything and came here Abraham but I am Scarlette's best friend and I am not going to tell you anything until and unless she wants me to do so. Therefore, stop trying to flirt with me, because for me, you are still Scarlette's ex-boyfriend. Better luck next time." She said bluntly and I was taken aback as she shook her head in denial.

I shrugged and went over to another girl who was staring at me, "Hey girl." I said to her and she seemed very much surprised, "Hi." She said fighting back a smile, "What is your name?" I asked her and she grinned cutely, "Renee Marcel." I held her hand which was very cold. "Call me soon." I whispered in her ear and handed her my card, by the expression on her face I could judge how happy she was before she nodded and took it from my hand.

Now Renee will take me Scarlette, or I must say, Saira. I smiled to myself and went back to where I was sitting just to see Scarlette looking at me but she quickly looked away as soon as our eyes met.

"Thank you everyone for coming and enjoying the event and for making it a grand success, we will be looking forward to see everyone tomorrow too. Thank you Believe in Magic for giving us the opportunity to host this beautiful event. Thank you Mr. Abraham Khan for granting us with pleasure by being here. Thank you to the sponsors and the parents of these beautiful children. Wish you have a good night and hope you come tomorrow also." After three long hours, she said wrapping up the first day of the event.

It was not as boring as I had thought it to be; in fact it was pretty impressive. Before I looked up Scarlette had already left the stage and Mrs. Braganza was coming over to me. "How did you find the event?" She asked me, "I absolutely loved it. Very impressive. The host was so good!" I blurted out the last line before face palming myself mentally, "Yes! Your friend, Saira Khan. She is such a life saver!" I chuckled mentally, "The original host Noel met with an accident. Saira being the sweetheart she is. She carried the entire event so nicely." She boasted.

"I want to meet your team! They are fabulous." I said to her, "Oh yes of course!" She squealed and started walking towards the backstage. "I was so nervous!" As we reached there I heard Scarlette speak while engulfed in a hug by Danielle and a blonde. "Girls, please listen." Mrs. Braganza announced and all of them straightened up, I noticed Scarlette holding Danielle's hand tighter causing Danielle to eye me.

"The young man here, Mr. Abraham Khan," She said pointing to me, "Ma'am please call me Abraham." I interrupted her and she nodded with a smile, "The young man here, Abraham, loved the hard work and dedication of you guys that made the event a success. He was very surprised to know that the host was changed in the last minute because Saira was as good as Noel," She said and pointed at her before she flashed her beautiful smile.

"You did so good Saira," I said putting emphasis on the name again, "Your first time is always the best." I said and I could sense her understanding what I actually meant, she bent her head down and closed her eyes before Danielle touched her shoulder, "Thank you Abraham." she muttered and I just smirked.

"Douche bag." I heard Danielle curse under her breath but I ignored it as no one else heard her.

"Oh dear you never told us Abraham Khan is your friend?" Mrs. Braganza asked her as she froze on her place, "Uh-" I interrupted her, "We met five years back so maybe she forgot to mention it." I then looked at her dead in the eye, "Maybe she forgot me." I said as sadness and emptiness took over me again.

"If any of you want pictures with him please come one by one," Mrs. Braganza interrupted my thoughts and all the girls except Danielle and her ran to where I was standing, "You want?" She asked Danielle but she shook her head in denial. She turned to walk away without looking back, leaving me alone just like she did five years back.

Chapter 26

<u>Scarlette</u>

"What was Abraham talking to you about when I was on stage?" I asked Danielle on call, "Uh nothing much! He was asking me about how I know you and everything." She replied. "Oh okay and what did you say?" I asked her unsurely.

"Relax babe, I said that I am your best friend and am not going to tell him anything until and unless you allow me to do so." She replied and a huge sigh of relief escaped my lips. "Now I think you must stop stressing over Abraham and go to sleep, you do not need to go on stage with dark circles, yeah?" She asked me and I chuckled.

"Yeah I do not want to look bad. We will meet tomorrow okay? Bye." I replied, "Bye, good night, I love you." She said in a cranky voice and I laughed, "I love you too."

I laid down on the bed, tired as hell by the long day after face timing my family and having a lot of beer to free my brain from Abraham. I had finally managed to ditch the looming black cloud that hung over my head and although I did not see clear blue skies yet, some of the clouds had gone away.

My home was on one side of Los Angeles while this place, where we were hosting the event, was on the other side. Travelling for 5 hours daily for three days was not a very nice idea so I rented a hotel room for these three days. As I was about to sleep there was a knock on the door, I checked my phone that flashed the time as 10 at night, I was so tired that even 10 o'clock seemed 1 o'clock to me.

I dragged myself to the door and opened to, "Who-" Suddenly a pair of lips locked with mine, taken aback yet I kissed him back because I guess I knew who he was. He pulled away breathlessly and I then opened my eyes to see him, looking in my eyes, his body pressed over mine and his tobacco smelling breath hitting my face.

"Abraham?" I tried to free myself from his grip but failed, "You remember me?" He said sarcastically, "Abraham please behave yourself. The door is open and all of my colleagues are living in the rooms next to me, I do not want you to create a scene that brings my job in danger." I scolded him.

Instead of going back he closed the door with one hand while he kept holding me with another. "Now the door is closed." He said and pulled me closer, I was under his spell when I realized what I was doing, "No, Abraham. This is not right." I freed myself from his grip and stood next to edge of the bed.

A familiar pair of hands snaked around my waist and his face was nuzzled in the crook of my neck, "I love you Scarlette." He whispered in my ears and I gave up, "I love you too Abraham." The atmosphere was quite, the only sound was of our heavy breaths and lips connected to each other.

My back was pressed on his chest while his hands travelled to my waist, pulling down the chain of my top because I had forgotten to bring my night clothes. He had opened it half when suddenly he stopped and closed it again, "What are you doing?" I asked him as he slowly secured the zip, "I do not want you to do something under the influence of alcohol that you regret later." He said and connected his lips with mine again.

He turned me around and his hands disappeared into my hair, his fingers twisting and pulling on the roots. My free hand rests on his waist, the kiss felt a little more intimate than the first. I got a weird fuzzy feeling at the pit of my stomach. Goosebumps flying up in my arms and spine.

A kiss is a lovely trick, designed by nature, to stop words when speech becomes nothing but superfluous.

He pulled away slowly, "I have to go." He whispered in my ears and turned to leave but I held his hand making him look back, "Don't go Abraham. I am nothing but a broken mess without you. I need you. I know what I did was the worst thing someone would do but I had no options. Stay back Abraham, stay here for the night. Please." I requested as tears were flowing down my cheeks, crying is the language of your heart when you are just too much filled up inside but lack words to spit it out.

"I will always be there for you." He pecked my cheek and engulfed me in a hug, in his arms lay my world yet I was the only person who had brought his world shattering down.

The memories of that night when I slept in his room returned flying back to my mind as he picked me up bridal style and laid me down on the bed. "Sing to me Abraham." I requested him and he chuckled before lying down next to me, putting his one arm around me while the other held my hand, "Now close your eyes angel." He spoke softly and kissed my head before starting the song, *our* song.

Next Morning

My eyes opened in annoyance as my I felt my phone vibrate, I tried to turn but felt something hold me back, looking down I saw a hand around my waist while my hands were intertwined with his. I jerked his hand away and sat straight, "Scar?" A sleepy Abraham's sexy voice filled my ears, "What are you doing here?" I yelled and he squinted his eyes at the sunlight with confusion evident on his face.

"You asked me to stay back." He stated simply, "No I remembered you put me to sleep but after that you should have left instead of cuddling with me!" I shouted while checking my clothes that were in place, "After putting you to sleep *you* did not leave my hand and *you* asked me to cuddle with *you*!" He shouted back putting emphasis on every single 'you' he spoke.

"You were the one who kissed me suddenly as you came!" I shouted.

"If I would have wanted I would have done many more things with you and you would have *never* known!" He shouted back.

"Oh my God! This proves what kind of brain you have! Who the hell gave you my address?" I asked him.

"I do not remember her name, it was something Rani…Rina…. but her surname of Marvel." He said and I face palmed, "That is Renne Marcel not Rina or Rani Marvel!" I exclaimed before he scratched his head, "Yeah, whatever, the same thing."

"Leave my room! Just leave right fucking now!" I yelled, "Give me a reason to do so." He crossed his arms. "I will not give you any reason!" I yelled at him, "Oh my God! I forgot! Scarlette Waters never gives reasons for doing anything. Right Ms. Waters?" He spoke with disgust and I casted my eyes at the floor.

Tears started welling up in my eyes, "Abraham," I sobbed, "You have no idea what my situation is and what my reasons were. I beg of you, please go from here. Please." I joined hands as tears started flowing out of my eyes. "You know what Scarlette?" He spoke with anger and disgust evident in his eyes, "Fuck off!" He yelled and left the room before closing the door with a loud bang.

I sat down on the floor as I kept crying at my destiny, "Why do I always have to hurt him for his good? Why am I always screwed by life?" I cried before I heard my phone vibrate again.

"*Augustus calling*," The Caller ID flashed on the screen. I clicked the receive button and pressed the phone to my ears, "Good morning Scarlette." He wished me. Augustus and Danielle were the only people after my family who were there for me through everything. Danielle knew everything while Augustus was the only person other than my family that was from my past.

"Good Morning Augustus." I wished as if everything was pretty normal, "Have you been crying?" He asked me in concern, "Yeah." I replied. "Oh yes, I saw in the newspaper that Abraham is the chief guest for your event." He spoke, "Much worse, I am the host because the original host Noel got into a car accident. Life sucks Augus!" I sighed. "Oh damn! That is not a very good thing but you get to see him after so long Scar!" He said excitedly.

"That is the worst part, I have to see him after what I did and he doesn't even know the reason. You know that." I sighed and as I looked up I saw an angry Abraham staring at me.

"A-Abraham?" I stuttered as I managed to get up, "So Augustus can know the reason and be with you while I cannot! What kind of a liar you are Scarlette? He can be in a relationship with you while it is bad for you to even see me for two days!" He yelled at me.

"No Abraham, it is not what you are thinking. Augustus is ju-"

"Oh of course it is what I am thinking! Had I not left my phone here, I would have never known!" He said and picked up his phone that was lying on the bed, "I hate you!" He yelled on my face and left the room.

"How on Earth can he talk to you like that?" Augustus yelled from the phone, "Shut up Augus! It is a thing between him and me. You need not interfere in it!" I yelled in anger and disconnected the call.

Every fucking thing in my life was screwed! And what the even worse thing was that I had to go to work today and host the remaining event.

Chapter 27

<u>Abraham</u>

Scarlette was very lost the whole day, she did not look at me even once since she came on the stage dressed in a Navy blue skin tight floor length gown with dark eye makeup and bright red lips.

As my performance ended she could not control her tears; she handed over the sheet of her speech to Renee, if that was her name, "Can you please take over the event from here? I am not feeling well." She told her and Renee nodded, "Okay, take rest." She smiled and confidently went up the stage.

Seeing her cry Danielle engulfed her in a hug and took her backstage, I quietly followed to see them going into a makeup room. "Hey, relax Saira. You need not cry. Shh!" Danielle said as she hugged her back comfortingly, "It sucks Danielle!" She yelled between her tears.

"I know it does," She replied, "No you do not! Because you are not going through it. Every single thing sucks in my life! It sucks to see Abraham's picture in the newspaper and not be able to talk to him, it sucks to see his depressed tweets on November 21st and February 14th and not be able to comfort him and tell him that I actually love him, it sucks and hurts to see him look at me with those eyes filled with hate. You know Danielle, once I had told him that I would never stay away from my family for someone else's sake but now I *am* living away…for his sake and it sucks that he has no fucking idea about it!" She covered her eyes with her fingertips, not caring about her make up getting smudged.

"The only source of happiness in my life is my family, just them and nothing else in the world." She cried more, "Okay, okay, want to face time home?" Danielle asked her and she nodded. "Then wipe your tears away, they will not like to see you like this. Cheer up sweetheart!" She rubbed her back and she nodded before taking a tissue paper and wiping off her smudged make up.

Danielle took out her phone and face timed someone, "Hello Augustus!" She chirped and I snorted in my brain at the mention of Augustus' name. "Hi Danielle. What's up?" He asked her, "Nothing dude. Scar is feeling homesick, are the others home?" She asked him and I guess he nodded.

She turned the screen towards Scarlette and what I saw shocked the hell out of me, "Mumma!" two little girls jumped in excitement on the screen and a warm smile crept up Scarlette's face, "Hey babies. How are you both?" She asked them.

"Mumma, Sarah is very bad." One girl pointed at the other one, "What did she do?" Scarlette asked him, "I was watching songs and she pushed me away and started watching Barbie movies!" She whined and both of them started pulling each other's hair, "Augustus, put them away!" Scarlette screamed between her laughter.

"Mumma when will you come?" The girl who I guess was Sarah whined on the screen, "Yes mumma, we miss you." The other girl too joined in, "Aww baby! Mumma misses her babies too but I have to work no? I will come back tomorrow in the morning." She said and both the kids jumped on the screen again.

She had this irresistible kind of light in her eyes and I could not believe she had her own children and she said she loved me yesterday. As soon as the call ended I barged into the room, "How could you do that?" I yelled and Scarlette froze as she saw me and slowly got up.

"What?" She blurted out.

"You have kids! Seriously?" I asked her and she looked down.

"They are adopted? Really?" I jumped with joy, "They are adopted, right?" I asked her but instead of agreeing she shook her head from side to side.

"They are my children. I have given birth to them." She said in a voice as low as a whisper.

My world came crashing down in those few seconds, "How old are they?" I asked her, "Five." She mumbled.

"And it has been five years since you left, you were not ready to marry me but you married Augustus and had two kids with him in the same year?" My pitch rose with every word I uttered. "No, you are taking it the wrong way. They are not Augustus' children." She said as her head shot up at my words.

"Whose kids are they?" I asked but she just looked down.

"Who is their father?" I asked again, this time a little louder.

"Whose kids are they?" I yelled.

"Yours!" She yelled back and I raised my eyebrows.

"Wh-what?" I blurted out.

"Yes Abraham Khan! I am the mother of your children and Augustus and Danielle helped me to bring them up." She spoke in anger but as soon as she completed a wave of shock went through her, her eyes went wide and she looked down again.

"How is this possible?" I asked her but she did not say anything. "Tell him Scarlette, please, he deserves to know." She rubbed her back. "No, I cannot." She buried her face in her hands and sat back on the chair.

"Please babe," I kneeled down in front of her and held her hands, "Please tell me, I want to know. Please Scarlette." She looked up at me and nodded.

"How is your mother?" She suddenly asked me, "My mother?" I asked her back and she nodded. I took a deep breath, "She is no more. She died in a car accident three years back." I closed my eyes as I realized no one close to me lived with me be it my parents or Sarah or Scarlette. "Did you notice any difference in her behavior in her last hours?" She asked me and I nodded, "She said I am sorry for what I did to Scarlette, Sarah and my gra. She was saying something else too but was never able to complete it." I sighed again as images of her dead self flashed in front of my eyes.

"Did you ever try to understand what she was saying or tried to find the reason to it?" She asked me and I shook my head in denial.

"I will tell you the reason," She said and paused, "Uh get up first, I do not want you to break your knees." I realized I was still on my knees and quickly got up.

"You remember a few days before Ashley and James' wedding I was very happy?" She asked me and I nodded. "I had missed my period, done my test and the result was positive. I was pregnant Abraham." She sighed, "Then why didn't you tell me baby?" I asked while cupping her face, "I wanted to tell you on Valentine's Day." She looked down again.

"Then on the day of the bridal shower I had gone early in the morning and when I came back my mood was off?" She asked me and I nodded.

"That day I went to get groceries and while returning, I saw your mom's car outside the Starbucks near our place. I stopped by and went inside to see her sitting.

"Hey Mrs. Khan, how are you?" I said as I tapped her shoulder, she turned around with a smile on her face, "Hello dear, I am good. How are you?" She asked me and I gave her a thumbs up in reply while she gestured me to sit in front of her.

"I have a really great piece of news to tell you!" I jumped on my seat in excitement, "Go on." She nodded while sipping her coffee, "I am pregnant." I said and she choked on her coffee after which I realized my words came out really weird. "You are what?" She asked me after coughing her lungs out, "Yes Mrs. Khan, your son is going to have a baby." This was better.

"Did you do the test?" She asked me worriedly and I found this pretty weird, "Yes I did and it is positive." I replied.

"Can we talk while I drive you home?" She asked me and I nodded suspiciously. She walked with me out to where her car was parked and opened the door of the passenger's seat for me to sit. She turned the ignition and the car roared to life.

"Now let me come directly to the point," She said and stopped the car in the side, "You have to get an abortion." She said simply and my jaw dropped on the floor. "Wh-" she raised her hand, "I have not finished yet," I nodded, "In our religion, having a child before marriage is considered as a sin. I cannot let my son be looked upon by the other people. Last time when I let him keep his baby our lives got ruined, I will not let you do that." She said and shook her head side to side.

"But I want to keep this child!" I cried, "No you will not!" She cried back.

"And what will you do?" I crossed my arms, "I can do many things Scarlette. Cheating allegations, accident, miscarriage…

anything." She said counting on her fingers, "This is your grandchild Mrs. Khan!" I cried and she rolled her eyes.

"Why do you think Sarah committed suicide?" She suddenly asked me, "Because she was hurt by Abraham's words." I shrugged but she shook her head side to side.

"No my love, that night after Abraham left her room I was there and had heard their conversation followed by Reyaan and Abraham's conversation. Why should my son bring up someone else's responsibility? I barged into her room only to yell at her and make her think that Reyaan is already not going accept the child but Abraham also will not accept it because he was not the father. She got so depressed by my words, that she killed herself. I am a very selfish person Scarlette, when Abraham was being blamed and insulted a part of me was dying but I did not confess anything because I had to bring up my two daughters. However, I do not have any purpose left now, my husband has died and my elder daughter is going to get married and once you leave…Abraham will bring Yasmin up. I can do anything now Scarlette." She threatened me and was very successful in threatening and intimidating me.

My world came collapsing down on my head; something for which you were blaming yourself all these years was never done by or because of you. The blame of her death had come on the person who loved the dead person the most whilst the actual murderer was drinking coffee at Starbucks.

"What kind of a person you are Mrs. Khan? You did all this to your son just because you are a selfish person? How could you do that to him? Do you even know how much he blames himself for Sarah's death?" I cried in disbelief and anger,

"Firstly lower your volume, secondly I do not care. It is better to feel sad for some time than to bring up a child till 17-18 years which was not even his." She shrugged heartlessly.

"I will keep this child, no matter what!" I said to her, she smirked, "And what if you have a miscarriage? Or what if you trip over something at your sister's bridal shower or wedding? Or what if you just fall down on your stomach as you get down from the car and walk to your home. Anything can happen anytime." She threatened me indirectly." She sighed and started crying again before I engulfed her in a hug.

I could not believe that my mother would do such a thing to me just for the sake of class and religion. She was the first lady I had fallen in love with and she was the one that threw me and my both lady loves apart. For the death I had been blaming myself all my life was not because of me and as I realized this a huge wave of relief went through my heart.

"Why didn't you tell me?" I asked her, "You had nothing except your family and I knew how much you loved your mother. I did not want to ruin your relations with her especially because you stayed with her for four and a half years before staying away for three and a half years. I remained quite all the time. I had to reject you for marriage that day because I did not want the first symbol of our love to die even before it took birth.

It broke my heart into a million pieces to see you shower me with your love because I was lying to you. I had to leave London and come here to Los Angeles because I knew you would never let me stay away from you and give birth to these children. I came to LA and started living with the name of

Saira Khan because once you told me that Saira was your favorite name.

I gave birth to our first children, who are twins, Sarah and Aashriya here; Augustus and Danielle were my first friends here and therefore they helped me in bringing them up. I left just after our last kiss because I knew I would not be able to see you cry and hurt just because of me. I did not fall into any relationship or even had a fling, let go getting married to someone; you were always on my brain and heart." She smiled, "They are no one else's but your children Abraham." I could not fight back the smile on my face.

"But why did you keep them? You should have aborted them, don't you love me?" I asked her, she shook her head, "I love you and that is love. Love is sacrifice. Love is sacrificing your needs for them. Love means you will always be there for them and not care about yourself but them. That is what I did Abraham." She looked down.

I had been blaming Scarlette for dumping me without an explanation when actually she was trying to save my children from dying even before their birth. Happiness filled my heart as I realized I was the father of two kids.

"Show me their picture." I shook her hand and she nodded before unlocking her phone and going through the gallery, "Uhm, uhm, uhm...this one." She said going through the pictures before stopping at one of them. She handed me her phone and I gasped at the cute sight that I saw, "Which one is who?" I asked her.

"The one in pink frock," She pointed to the black haired girl who had her eyes like me while the other features as same as Scarlette, "She is Aashriya." She pointed to the other back haired girl who looked as same as me, in fact she looked like the childhood version of me with longer hair, "The one in red frock is…Sarah." She smiled at me.

"They are so cute!" I said like a girl, "They are your daughters!" She replied with a giggle. "You know what? They are very different from each other. While Aashriya plays with cars and video games, Sarah plays with Barbie dolls and teddy bears. Yet both of them love Groove songs, though I have not let them watch any music videos because that would make them find similarities between you and them but they are in love with the songs." She spoke with this undeniable light in her eyes.

I could not help but wrap my arms around her waist as I pulled her in for a kiss, the rise and fall of her chest and the sound of her heartbeat managed to make me forget about things for a little while.

"Happy ending bitches!" We were startled by Danielle's voice and claps, "I was still standing, in case you forgot." She shrugged and excused herself before winking at Scarlette.

I quickly kneeled down, "Scarlette Waters," I spoke and held her hand before judging the surprised expression on her face, "I cannot imagine growing old with anyone else, nor do I want to." She covered her mouth with her other mouth, "This is actually happening?" She asked and I nodded.

"I know you are the only one I want to share my imperfections with for the rest of my life Scarlette Waters. The story of our love is only beginning. Let us write our own happy ending... So in short, will you please marry me Scarlette?" I repeated the same lines as the ones I had said to her that day.

"Because I love you. I am in love with you and I want you to hold me forever, and wake up next to every morning. And I want to be friends with you, and be committed to you. Because I am really fucking sorry, and I hope you will be able to forgive me for blaming you forever. Maybe not today, but someday, I know you will forgive me. And I can wait, I can just wait outside in the pouring rain, I will wait in the dark for you, I will break my spleen for you. I want you and my kids the most in the world Ms. Waters. Will you please change your surname officially from Waters to Khan? Will you be my Mrs. Scarlette Abraham Khan?" I said and looked up at my world.

"Yes." She said excitedly as tears of pure joy and happiness welled up in her eyes, "Yes I do Abraham Khan." She said before I kissed her ring finger and she bent down and connected her lips with mine.

"Saira where di-" Mrs. Braganza stared at us wide eyed before we quickly pulled away, "Did I interrupt something?" she said looking at both of us and having a hard time fighting back a smile, "I am sorry and...Congratulations." She smiled and left before closing the door behind her and we blushed madly.

"I want to meet Sarah and Aashriya." I said and she nodded, "Same story!" she chuckled along with me. "Let's go." I said and started to walk away, "I am not going in a lavish navy blue gown, let me change." She laughed a bit.

"Change." I crossed my arms, "Shut up and go." She said before pushing me out while laughing.

After a while she came out in a navy green top, an off white pencil fit knee length skirt and black heels, I could not help but whistle, "You do not look like a mother of two kids, my love." She widened her eyes before blushing.

After bidding adieu to everyone we drove to her hotel room, collected her things and then drove to her house after a tiring two hour drive.

On reaching, she rang the bell, "Who is-" Augustus said opening the door, "Scarlette!" He grinned wide happily before pulling her in a hug, "Abraham?" He spoke with confusion evident in his voice, "He knows." She mumbled and he nodded before letting us in.

"Mumma!" Sarah and Aashriya ran in our direction looking super cute in white and pink frocks, "My babies!" She kneeled down to their level and hugged them together, "We missed you." Sarah said to her. "I missed my little angels too, that is why I came running back." She said causing them to giggle.

"Who are you?" Sarah asked me, "You do not talk to a guest like this, stupid." Aashriya said before hitting Sarah's head and causing a WWF match between each other. As she said 'stupid' Scarlette shot a glare in Augustus' direction which meant that she was pretty conservative.

"What is your name?" Aashriya asked me adorably after Scarlette pulled them away from each other, "My name is Abraham Khan." I introduced myself but she frowned, "Why do you look like Sarah?" She tilted her head side to side when

Sarah too joined in and started touching my face, as if checking I was real.

"Sarah and Aashriya, remember I told you that your father has gone on a trip to moon to bring gifts for his angels?" Scarlette asked them and they nodded in reply, "He has come back." She said and both the kids jumped happily. "Where is dad?" Sarah asked in excitement. Scarlette smiled and pointed at me before both the kids stared at me with confusion.

"He is your father." She said and both the kids smiled at each other before hugging me quickly, "Dad why did you take so long to come back?" Sarah asked me. "I could not find the perfect gift for my little fairies." I said and held their hands.

"What did you bring?" Aashriya asked and I kissed both their cheeks, "Dad could not find anything better than his fairies." I pouted but instead of nagging they smiled, "It is okay. We are smart girls, we understand. We just wanted you!" Sarah said and both of them hugged me again.

I looked around to see Scarlette smiling at us while Augustus was putting a ring box in the drawer as a tear drop fell on his hand. As I could see my world starting; I could also see another world ending, one that could not even start.

Scarlette

Abraham, Sarah and Aashriya got along so well, it almost made me cry. "Augustus you want to eat something?" I turned to him but he shook his head, "Anyone else?" I asked to my three children.

"I am hungry mumma!"

"Me too mumma!"

"Me three mumma!"

"Wasn't that funny?" Abraham asked as he raised out his palm and both of them high fived it.

After getting married in Los Angeles itself, we returned back to London. Everyone was married, to my surprise; Ellie was expecting her second child with Jacob because her first time ended in a miscarriage. My mother had died with cancer that was detected only when it was in its final stage.

Yasmin was engaged to an American singer called Austin while Adina and Leona were expecting their second child. Adina's first child was a daughter called Ada and Leona's first child too was a daughter called Salma. Alisha was a successful DJ in a night club; she was engaged to a businessman called Mike O'Neil.

I started living my life with my original name, Scarlette Abraham Khan because my children, Sarah Khan and Aashriya Khan had found their father who literally brought them up like his little angels.

PROLOGUE

50 years later

"I will never forget that day at the hospital, when we were on tour." He chuckled softly, stoking my white fragile hair.

"Either." I giggled as he kissed my forehead.

Maria, my little child came running.

"Grandma! Grandma! Grandma!" She shouted.

"Yes baby where is your mumma? I smiled, fixing her braid weakly.

"She is with dad. She told me to leave them alone a little bit." She pouted cutely.

"Aww! And where is Ada aunt?" I asked her.

She tilted her head in thought, "Ada aunt has gone out with her kitty party friends." She pouted again.

"Aww my poor baby left all alone? Hahaha come here." I giggled.

"No I am going to stay with granddad!" She stuck her tongue out at me and ran towards Abraham.

He high fived her little hands and winked at me "See Scarlette? She wants to stay with me. Now you be jealous!"

I just laughed and looked at my wheelchair for a while, then posed my head on his shoulder silently.

"Alright Maria look who is here! Go play with her!" He pointed at Maria's best friend Angela.

She giggled "Okay!" and ran away.

I enjoyed Abraham's warm embrace for the last tiny moments and closed my eyes not to open them anymore after, with a smile on my face. I am proud to say that I spent my life with a man who treated me like an amazing wife; he took care of me like no one did before.

I am so proud of him, I am so proud of myself and I am so proud of us that we did not life and fate's conspired little games kill us but we stayed strong in this game of love versus fate and became infinite.

Yes I am proud to say it: Everything started when I thought I was dying and that was the moment when I found my life in Abraham Khan.

He will soon notice that I am not going to open my eyes, that I had left and certainly he will join me soon. I cannot believe I hated him before I was lying on that hospital bed, while almost giving up on life.

I love you so much, I love you death.

I wanted you to stay with me until my last breath and be my infinity.

And you did, Thank You Abraham Khan.

I love you till infinity.

ABOUT THE AUTHOR

Eishita is a Lucknow (India) based fourteen-year-old girl hailing from a family of avid readers and travelers. She continues the legacy. Barely into her teens, Eishita is passionate about dance, dramatics, travelling and writing. She is a trained Bharatanatyam dancer. This 5 feet 10 inches girl wrote her first novel "How Could I Not See Him?" at a tender age of twelve. Her loyalties  are towards romantic fiction with a tinge of sarcasm. She calls herself "a love story addict" and sagacious

Stay connected with Eishita on her Facebook account www. facebook.com /eishita.pretty, follow her on Twitter (@EishitaMisra), Instagram (@Eishita_Official) and Wattpad (@TheTallTeenager)